Sometimes, Love Just Won't Let Go

Sometimes, Love Just Won't Let Go

A Novel

Ashaki Boelter

Shakalot High Entertainment

Sometimes, Love Just Won't Let Go

Library of Congress

Cataloging-in-Publication Data

ISBN: 978-0-9796219-9-4

Sometimes, Love Just Won't Let Go

Written by Ashaki Boelter

All Illustrations by Ashaki Boelter

Printed in the USA by Lulu Publishing

Published by Shakalot High Entertainment, 2020

Edited: In-House Shakalot High Entertainment

Dedicated to...

My family and friends

I want to take a second to thank all of those readers who can stomach it through to the end of this wild and crazy story.

TABLE OF CONTENTS

x

By Ashaki Boelter

Chapter 1

Do You Have Drugs?

Above the rooftops of various industrial buildings sat the monotonous moon, the only object in the midnight scene that did not shake in the rearview mirror to the base-bumping tweeters of a resurrected 1978 Olds Cutlass Supreme. Love of an outdated, an old classic was just too hard to let go of because, as the saying went, nothing ever beat an original. Why fake the funk, when all you had to do was put some dirt-cheap tire caps that old junk to flex the love?

"Sometimes, love just won't let go."

Loc'd after dark, under glimmering stars, Vern Mayes and Keyshawn Jackson cruised away from a hard night's work of stowing, scanning, and delivering heavy packages from a warehouse. The sudden thought to rush home and sleep did not seem like the best of plans. They had the next few days off from work, and their

1

suffocating girlfriends were out of town for a week, as of yesterday. Vern and Keyshawn were free, cool, calm, and in collections but would never answer those calls because that was another story!

No, this was a love story centered on what happens when others influenced a relationship, and the direct lovers took advice on how it should have looked. How could people be so gullible to live another person's fantasy instead of their own? Starting today, Keyshawn and Vern were in the clear. No more instructions, no more orders, and no more nagging from not just their girlfriends, but from family, from the church, and indeed the press.

Keyshawn slowly spun his wool-covered steering wheel with one wrist, as his magnificent Cutlass dipped and tilted around a corner. He marveled at his furry black dice that swung below his rearview mirror but objected to the bird dropping that slithered down his window, a translucent dread of an incurable love story that would come upon him. Keyshawn needed to keep his eyes on the road ahead, but unfortunately, with blinding shades, he missed the warning signals.

Suddenly, Vern had a flash of what they could do! "Aye bro, let's get hammered tonight like we used to do. Know what I'm saying? Let's hit downtown and roll up to the Golden Whale Club."

"If our girlfriends find out, they'll kick our ass when they get back home," replied Keyshawn, as he removed his shades and pierced Vern's adolescent brain. "Mines told me that she wants us to get away from all that, and she said your girlfriends said the same."

"Fuck them' bitches," Vern declared. "We got to do what we do. Know what I'm saying? They want to go on those church trips, but yet we can't do what we want? What's up with that? So, since we haven't done much but work all week, we are going to the club tonight and do a bunch of drinking and dancing! We're going to have fun!"

"Yeah, you're right!"

"Can I get an Amen?"

"Well."

"They just left town for an entire week, so let's take advantage of our guy time! There won't be any nagging for an entire week."

"Preach on, brother!"

2

"There won't be no' drama about taking out the garbage!"

"Well!"

"We can piss all over the toilet seat and not worry about cleaning it up for the rest of the week!"

"That's right!"

"We can do whatever and go wherever we want!"

"See, that's how you're going to get me into trouble with Veronica, thinking like that."

Yes, Keyshawn and Vern had girlfriends. *Fortunately,* Veronica and Rochelle left today to be out of town for a week to renew themselves at a revitalizing women's church retreat at a resort in Atlanta, which was sponsored by several black churches across our fabulous country.

Vern was excited. "We're going to get blasted tonight!"

"I don't know, Vern. Now that I think about it, I think you are a drink away from being an alcoholic! You've got no control of it when your girlfriend is not around. Maybe we should skip a club tonight. You don't handle your liquor very well in clubs, and I'm not up to all the assistance when you mess up."

"Whatever, dude! Look Key. We're hitting the club tonight. Know what I'm saying? I got this tonight. Go on, and you drop me off at home real' quick and then in about an hour, pick me up. And I sure hope that Earl Mack is there tonight too. He's supposed to be in town all weekend!"

"Earl Mack, the luckiest gambler we've ever seen, is here?"

"Yep, he sure is."

"That's the only dude, I know, that gets away with sporting a 3-2-1 Contact, Theo shag after 1990. And I heard that he was on televised poker shows last year. Is he still out there like that?"

"Yep, he's still making a grip. He's famous!" Vern was envious. "Know what I'm saying? He owns a castle in Malibu, like sixteen exotic cars, and takes a lot of oversea trips with the hottest strippers, while sporting a played out that 3-2-1 Contact, Theo shag. The man has got it going on, so you can't knock the hairdo!"

"So, what brings him back home these days?"

"My ex-girlfriend, La Donna, attends the same church as his momma." He looked over his shoulder as if he was suddenly deep in thought about a secret mission or conversation. "She told me the other day that they've been doing special offerings to help with his momma's medical expenses. I guess she's gotten old and sick, over there coughing and spitting up shit at home. I don't know what her deal is. It sounds like she's a hot mess, I guess."

"But hold up! What's up with you talking to *La Donna*?"

"La Donna and I broke up many years ago, playa. We're just friends! Know what I'm saying? Besides, she's not that *ho* like before; she's working on cleaning up her life. Despite what you see on the blocks, she's a Christian nowadays; she goes to church."

Keyshawn rolled his eyes. "I thought Christianity had rules?"

"They do. At least, that is what this one pastor preached to me the last time he outdrank me at this bar."

"A pastor drank with you? He must've hurried his message."

"Hey, Jesus drank." Vern rolled his eyes back at Keyshawn. "The pastor stopped preaching the moment he felt tipsy. It's all good."

"Is that what the Bible says, that you can drink until drunk?"

"I don't know; I'm not a church scholar." Vern smacked his lips. "Man, anyways, Rochelle is my gal! Know what I'm saying? She doesn't have to know anything because there isn't anything to it, bro. La Donna is just a friend these days!"

"Rochelle is going to come back from that church conference and kill you when she finds out you're still talking to your hooker ex when she's out of town!"

"She's not going to find out, and you're not going to say anything about it to your gossip column gal. This conversation goes nowhere else! Do you got' that?"

"Why are you yelling at me? I wouldn't put your business on blast. And I didn't say you did anything; I was just wondering."

"Just because she's a hooker doesn't make her a bad person."

"I guess."

Vern could not resist. "Keyshawn, have you seen her recently out there on the blocks? La Donna has been in the gym, and now she's blossomed! I'm a mammal; man, by nature, I got to look!"

"How could anyone miss her? She's always standing there flirting at the corner of 5th and Mission Boulevard."

Vern licked his lips. "Honestly, she's still got those fat, lip popping, big hypnotic, succulent, and juicy extra-African melons that I used to drool over. Know what I'm saying?"

"I try not to look."

"Everybody looks. Whenever I leave the chicken joint across the street from where La Donna flaunts, sometimes I just sit in my car and reminisce the times I used to tear it up for free every day!"

"Like that?"

"Like that, Keyshawn. She paid me for some loving!"

"Bro, you need to let go of all that. You've moved on."

"Keyshawn, Sometimes, Love Just Won't Let Go! Know what I'm saying? Maybe you don't. I do love Rochelle, but she's becoming a nun or something. I'm not there. The jury is still out for Rochelle. But, you and your gal got a good thing, and there isn't any way you're losing her to feel the pain I had with losing La Donna."

"Enough already," said Keyshawn, who shook his head. "If Rochelle finds out you're talking to your ex, especially La Donna, she's liable to cut your ass! Despite her getting her life together with the Lord, Rochelle is still straight ghetto!"

"I know."

"Uh-huh."

"Don't hate the player, Keyshawn; hate the *game*!"

"I'd be shocked if you and Rochelle last another week."

"Women are a dime a dozen. Know what I'm saying? They're here today and *gone* tomorrow! Rochelle is life now, but La Donna is simply *kitty cat* insurance, player!"

"You're crazy to have some chick in your back pocket."

"Whatever, dude." Vern looked at his watch. "All I'm saying *now* is that tonight, Earl Mack will be down and out over his sick momma. He'll drink, get drunk, and gamble until he passes out. Know what I'm saying? Homies told me that people could get three months of rent out of him when he's drunk. So stop with the relationship jazz and stab the gas!"

Keyshawn placed a little pressure on the accelerator pedal to speed up their ten-mile travel through nothing but smelly farms.

"Come on, Keyshawn! Are you an old fart or something?"

"I'm not trying to get pulled over tonight. Cops, they hide behind bushes on this road, all the time."

"You're just chicken. Put some stank on it!"

"I ain't no' damn chicken!" Keyshawn stabbed the gas, and off the 78' Olds Cutlass flew!

"We're going back through time!" celebrated Vern. He rolled down the window. "We're doing warp drive now, captain!"

"100 miles per hour, baby! Now, roll that window back up because it smells like some kind of poisoned manure out there!"

"But aye Keyshawn, check it out ahead in the road. It looks like an animal or something. You might want to go around whatever that is. Go around it, bro!"

"What is it? I don't see anything! Where do you see it?"

"It's right there!"

"Where is it?"

Blast! Dump! Dump! Dump!

"Ooh shit!" Vern looked back. "You ran it over!"

"What was it?"

"I don't know! All I see is chunks and nuggets coming from the tires and puddles of guts. And don't you even think about stopping to check it out; we've seen that movie before. I ain't the one!"

"Whatever it was, it made my transmission slip. Are you sure it wasn't like... a human?"

"It wasn't human, Keyshawn. It was an animal."

6

Ka-dunk!

"What was that?"

Vern assured. "That was the head that just came out from underneath the car. Nope, it wasn't human for sure. It might have been a goat or something. I don't know. It is crow-feed now, though!"

About a mile back, a farmer that wore bargain overalls, plaid shirt, and straw hat stood in the middle of the road. His nostrils flared, as tobacco smoke exited into the wind. He sealed his lips upon an inherited pipe until he said, "Bertha, hand me the damn flashlight!"

His wife waddled to him, as they watched the red rear lights of Keyshawn's Cutlass disappear into the far darkness. "Here you go, daddy. Yikes! What is all the sticky stuff on the road?"

"Let me take a look here, Bertha." The husband slapped the old flashlight a few times to stop the flickering light. Finally, the bright beam settled. "Good God Almighty, it's our pig!"

Bertha cried out, "Good golly, daddy! His guts are all over the ground for yards. He didn't deserve to get run over!"

"Damn it! That car was going too fast through here!"

Bertha comforted her husband. "I should certainly go and call the cops, daddy! That's what I'll do. I'll call the sheriff!"

"Those city bastards are going to pay for this, driving around here like some kind of lunatics!" The husband's face turned completely red. "I know it was one of those thugs, driving all the time through here with their lowriders, and that wretched rap music!"

"Daddy, is that *poor* Dilbert's head next to your foot?"

7

The farmer held his pipe and looked down. Dilbert's decapitated head faced him; its squashed eyes stared back at him! The disgusted farmer angrily punted the pig head into a nearby ditch, as its eyeballs rolled off his steel toe boots!

"Look at all this shit!" The farmer searched the entire area and realized that Dilbert's guts splattered all over the street, ran in the ditches, slimed up the trees, and across the harvest and crops. Everything looked as if it was saturated with orange seasoning salt and sprinkled with bits of blackberries! "I'll be damned if somebody isn't going to pay for this!"

"Now, calm down, daddy. You'll have another one of those strokes if you get too bothered!"

"That is the second pig in a month that some black or brown degenerate has run over! I see them roasting through here at speeds of over 100 miles per hour all the time! I've called in license plates way too many times, and I'm sick and tired of this!"

"Calm down, daddy! We'll just go inside and call the police."

"The police won't do a damn thing," he continued, "so, cut the gas. I think it is about time that I pull out my old man's shotgun from the attic; I'll find my stinking justice! Do you got' that?"

Bertha quickly ran into the house and called the police before her husband could take matters into his own hands.

A few miles down that very road, now into the downtown business district of their city, Keyshawn skid his Cutlass around a wet street corner and lost a tire cap on the straightaway!

"This part of town is always dead at night. There's nobody out here. Hold on to your seat, homeboy!"

"Man, you had better slow this car back down!"

"You just asked me to floor it! Oh, so you can't hang now?"

"I thought I saw a cop back there, Keyshawn."

Whoop! Whoop! There went the sound of the police.

"Shit!" Keyshawn slowed his car down and removed his sunglasses. He hadn't seen the red and blue lights until now!

Vern simply melted into his seat.

"My cell phone is in my jacket in the trunk! Do you have yours, Vern?"

"I'm on it!" Vern pulled his cell from his pants pocket, but he dropped it down the side of the seat. "Oops! I don't know where it fell! Know what I'm saying? I can't find it!"

"Dude!" hollered Keyshawn. "Your phone slid under your seat! See if you can reach it! Hurry up, dude. I got to pull over!"

"I can't reach it! I don't feel it!"

Whoop! Whoop!

"Pull over!" The police shouted through the squad car speakers. "Pull over now in the name of the law!"

Keyshawn pulled over to the side of the road and shut off his car engine. He tried to watch the police in his rearview mirror, but they shined their spotlight directly into his car. He couldn't see anything except blinding white lights and colorful stars.

"Good evening, boys," greeted the cop, who stood at the driver's side door. He was overly confident with that gun at his side, as his arrogant partner secured Keyshawn's passenger door. Even though their squad car spotlight nearly lit up the planet, both cops still beamed their flashlights into the driver and passenger's faces.

"What did I do?" Keyshawn gripped his steering wheel with both hands. "Sir, what did I do?"

"Are you kidding me?" The cop chuckled. "Do you realize how fast you were driving this old piece of garbage?"

"This is a classic, sir!"

"Well. Do you realize that you also drove your *classic* over somebody's pig back there? Huh?"

"Is that what it was?" Vern blurted in laughter. He looked that cop dead in the eye. "Did we hit your cousin?"

"He didn't mean it!" Keyshawn immediately shook his head.

"For the love of..." the cop was suddenly pissed off. "Pass me your damn license and registration right now, boy! And you over there, I want you to shut your damn yap if you know what's good for

9

you! There is nothing funny about running over a pig or insinuating that a cop is a pig! Do I make myself clear, boy? I'm the law!"

"Dang dude... You need to calm down." Vern puckered.

"Here you are, sir." Keyshawn kindly handed his license and registration to the cop. "I'm sorry about my friend. He had a long week at work. Just do your job, and we will be on our way."

Vern spat, "What? Keyshawn, you don't have to apologize for me! Know what I'm saying? These hillbilly cops can't take a joke!"

"Your name is Keyshawn?" The irritated cop ignored Vern. "You look familiar to me. Wait a second. I know you. You're the fellow whose girlfriend used to date the professional baseball player, aren't you? She's the big-time journalist, Veronica Evans!"

"Yes! That's my girlfriend."

"Yeah, I've read about you in magazines," said the police officer. "Miss Evans always mentions you in articles about how much she loves you. Keyshawn, you're one lucky son of a bitch! Frankly, I don't know how you scored that sexy and wealthy woman, and still drive a piece of crap like this."

The other cop chuckled along. "I don't know either, but what I do know is that Veronica Evans has one hell of a body! I know what I'd be doing every night with that. I wouldn't be out here driving around like losers; I'd be at home doing it to her all night long."

"Excuse me, but you don't get to talk about what you would do with my friend's girlfriend." Vern was done with the candidly abusive law enforcement. "You're an asshole, man."

"Is that so?" The partner cop took a step back and placed his finger on the gun that sat in his holster. "Repeat it, boy! I dare you!"

"Wait!" Keyshawn watched the trigger-happy police officer get aggressive at his friend's window. "Thanks for all of the compliments, officer. Are we good now? Can we go?"

The officer at Keyshawn's window said, "Stand down, Officer. I just need to get this fellow's proof of insurance."

"Why?" asked the partner cop. "If he doesn't have insurance, would you want this piece of crap in our yard? Look at those cheap caps on the tires. It looks like he's missing one; this car has no value. I guess it goes to say that sometimes, love just won't let go."

Keyshawn kindly handed the cop whatever he wanted. "Here you are, officer."

"And you too," said the cop that leaned on the passenger side door. "I'd like to see your identification card, too, rap star."

"Well, I don't have any I.D. on me, man." Vern replied, "Know what I'm saying? I'm clean! Just don't shoot me!"

"I'm not going to shoot you," stated the cop, who took a deep breath. "Now, kindly tell me, what is your name?"

"Wait! Don't hit me with that stick! Ah! Ouch!"

"Boy, have you been drinking, or are you on something?"

"Boy?" Vern looked around. "I don't see any boys around here! I'm a grown-ass man, dude! Know what I'm saying? You'd better ask somebody! Shit. I ain't the one, punk-ass cop."

"You have an attitude problem. Now, tell me your name!"

"No!"

"No?"

"Did I stutter?"

"You little gangster shit," replied the cop. He copped an attitude even more farce and pulled his pistol out. He had no filter. "You'd better answer my question. Should I call you Jerome or Abdul? Tell me, or I'll shoot that stupid-looking grin off your face!"

Vern was amused. "Okay, I surrender! My name is Richard."

"Okay, Richard, what is your last name?"

"Sir, my name is Richard Whiteman."

"Oh my god," muttered Keyshawn. He melted into his seat.

"Keyshawn Jackson and Richard Whiteman, where are you two headed?" asked the cop, who bought Vern's phony name. He placed his gun back into his holster. "As fast as you guys were going, it must be an important destination. We want to know."

11

"Just issue a ticket for goodness sake so that we can be on our way!" Keyshawn was done. "I was speeding, but there isn't any need to be harassing us over some stupid pig that walked onto the dark road. Maybe suggest that whoever the hell's pig-owner is, close his damn gate, so his dumbass animals don't escape. That wasn't my fault!"

Vern looked at his watch again. "Can you police hurry up with the speeding ticket? Shit."

"We will be right back." The irritated cops, with their fingers on their triggers, walked back to their squad car to check out Keyshawn's information in their dashboard computer and eat donuts.

One of the cops waved to a set of approaching headlights and shouted, "These boys are perfect! Come on!"

"I wonder why the cops have reinforcements pulling up behind us." Keyshawn noticed that a van pulled up and several men jumped out. "For real, though, I think we might be in some serious trouble out here! Four... five... six... There's like ten dudes coming to my car!"

Vern was suddenly scared. "Keyshawn, drive this bitch!"

Both cops returned.

"You two hoodlums step out of the vehicle right now," ordered one cop. "Slowly get out of your car, and nobody gets shot!"

"What?" Keyshawn was like, what's up.

"Hell to the no, I ain't getting out the car!" Vern quickly locked his door. "Forget that! Look at all those cops out there! Know what I'm saying? Keyshawn, you'd better start this damn car!"

The cop at Keyshawn's door pulled out his gun and pointed it towards him! "Don't even think about it. I said to get out now, boy!"

"Hey sir, now we don't want any trouble," said Keyshawn, as he cautiously opened his door. "Hold on! Be cool guys; we're getting out. I know I was speeding and that I ran over a pig, but this is fucking ridiculous, man!"

A third cop yelled, "Put your hands up! Shut your mouth and lay on the ground! Turn on your stomach! Put your hands behind your head!" He proceeded with the Miranda Rights.

"Hey, we're on television," whispered Vern. He noticed the camera crew. "What's up with this? Oh, snap! We're being taped for the television show, Police Tales!"

A nearby cop had makeup blotched onto his face. He was immersed in his lines, while his fellow officer walked up to Keyshawn and Vern. The cameraman followed.

"Am I on?" The fellow officer cleared his throat and gave his *good-guy* speech into the camera.

"Roll it!" shouted a director. "You're on, officer!"

"In the bay area, this is what the streets are like daily." The police officer used a deep voice and raised his chin. "I do this every night to keep the streets clean and quiet for you and your families. Thugs like these think like wild animals and think these streets are their jungle."

"I ain't no' animal!" Vern shouted.

The director noted to edit that comment out.

Meanwhile, the star cop was pleased with his articulation of the crime scene. "I'm here for the people of our county to continue to make it the safest place to live on the planet. I grew up here, and the last thing I want to happen is for these young gangster thugs to tear down what I helped to build with my well-earned college degrees, dreams, and prayers to the good Lord above."

"Hey, cop!" Keyshawn interrupted. "I didn't do anything but drive fast and run over a jaywalking pig! All you had to do was simply issue a fucking ticket! You didn't have to film all this shit!"

"Hey!" shouted the cop. "We're trying to film here, and this is a family show! So, shut the fuck up!"

Vern blurted, "You should've just driven off, Keyshawn!"

Keyshawn tugged for his freedom but was helpless. "Somebody help us! They're harassing us!"

"Cut! Cut!" cried the director. "What the hell! Will someone please shut them up? They aren't the damn victims here!"

"Somebody call a civil rights leader about these crooked cops!" Keyshawn cursed. "This is some racist bullshit!"

"Shut that man up!" The director lost it. "Put some tape over his mouth! That's it. Thank you! Now, let us add a little action out here, so we don't bore the hell out of our viewers. Grab his arm or something. We need more flare and violence! Now, roll it!"

In seconds, a dust cloud covered three cops and Keyshawn. While on his back, he gave the police a real fight with his feet. However, a dog pile of cops ensued, and Keyshawn surrendered.

"Do you have drugs in the car?" asked a police officer.

The young friends were indeed in some serious mess. Three cops now circled Vern like a pack of lions around a wildebeest. Keyshawn, with tape over his mouth to stop him from talking, was dragged away from his car to begin a sobriety test.

"We just found a few bags of cocaine in the car," explained a cop directly into the television camera. "Also, these gentlemen were driving around with an illegally opened bottle of alcohol, which appears to be your typical forty ounces you'd find in the car of most gangster Negroes in our city of..."

The director shouted, "Cut! You can't say *Negroes* on our Police Tales show! You stick to the script, or else I'll recast you, you dipstick! Now, do the scene again. Roll it!"

"But he is a Negro," explained that cop. "Ask him if he calls himself that too. I bet he does! They all do!"

"You cannot say that word!" shouted the director. "Roll it!"

"Dude is an ass!" Vern blurted, "That cop, like a lot of them around here, is nothing but a bigot! Don't edit anything; let the world see and hear the truth! Please, let the truth set us free!"

"Also, there's an open bottle of alcohol in the back seat," continued the cop into the camera upon a second take. "It appears to be your *typical* forty ounces you'd find in the car of most bay area thugs. Also, I want to point out that while the passenger is restrained, the driver is over there, failing the standard sobriety test. We cops believe that this kind of work saves lives and makes the world a better place. We are here to protect you and serve our county."

"But we haven't been drinking!" Vern shouted, "Keyshawn is over there, failing the sobriety test because the cops just whooped his ass! Know what I'm saying? Besides, why don't you try to say ABC's backward with cameras on you and around ten suckers that want to kick your ass and shoot you down?"

"Don't hate the players, bad boys," whispered the cop, "hate the game. Our country is in a recession, and acting puts extra money in a cop's pocket. I have bills and mouths to feed! So, you play along, or else I'll find you outside of all this television business and give you something to worry about."

"I heard that, and we'll be editing that out, deputy!" The director felt hopeless. "You're not a gang member, officer. You're a cop! Please, remember that you do have a boom microphone above you. Now, keep rolling! I need more flare and energy! For goodness sake, where are the police dogs? Now, let's go on to the next scene. What's next? Go to the coke page! If you know the lines, go on!"

"So," continued the partner cop, who tasted the white flower from the sandwich bag in his hands, "is this your cocaine?"

15

"What?" Vern looked at the cop and flipped him off! "No, that ain't my shit! You can get out of here with that mess. Know what I'm saying? You can kiss my ass! "

The other cop ruggedly dragged Keyshawn back over against his car, right next to Vern, and ripped the tape from this mouth.

Rip!

"Ouch! That hurt, man! Damn!"

"Then is this your cocaine, Keyshawn Jackson?"

"You guys planted that! It belongs to your momma!"

"Cut!" The director was livid. "This isn't Perry Mason or Matlock! Stop all the questions, and let's get to the action before I fall asleep! Now, unlock one of their handcuffs! Let him run away!"

The cops were stumped.

"Television viewers love good cop chases when it involves black people," answered the director. "Then add the police dog, and it is a wrap for ratings! Anybody that channel surfs will stop on our show. Somebody make sure the helicopters are in place. Okay! Everyone in place! Roll it!"

"Forget that! I ain't running!" Those were Keyshawn's infamous and untelevised last words before he was roughly helped to his feet by the police. They shoved him forward!

16

"Cut!" The director then signaled for a black stunt actor to run past Keyshawn. "Roll it!"

Local law enforcement, Vern, and Keyshawn stood there and watched a local stuntman, dressed just like Keyshawn, start out stumbling and run about twenty yards and hop over a fence, before being tripped up and gnawed on by the police dog!

The acting police officers shot at, clubbed, stunned, and apprehended the Keyshawn actor with fake weapons. Seconds later, the cameras turned back on towards the real cursing Keyshawn and Vern, who got handled and stuffed into the back of a squad car.

After filming, the cops laughed it up, as Keyshawn and Vern were taken straight to jail that night. They never got theatrically crazed, did drugs, or got violent as the scheduled show portrayed, but only they knew that.

A night of restlessness, Keyshawn and Vern awoke to a jail guard that said they were free. Keyshawn's girlfriend, Veronica Evans, paid the bail. She angrily dragged her boyfriend and his friend out of the precinct, in Jesus name.

"I was miles away praising the Lord!" Veronica screamed at Keyshawn. "I got some call from one of my publicist saying that you got arrested last night! Then my boss calls me! None of this looks good; I've got a reputation to hold! I left town to focus my life and grow closer to God. Is this the kind of thing I can come to expect from you, Keyshawn? If it is, I cannot be or grow into what I can be!"

Keyshawn replied, "I'm sorry. I guess I got a little lippy with the cop. We're both sorry. I love you, Veronica."

"I love you too," said Veronica. "Let's go."

"I cannot believe it," whispered one of the cops that arrested the two friends last night. He stood there at the precinct doors with another officer. "They ran over a pig, sped through the city, and back-talked us during their citation. They're leaving after not even a full day. I bet they think they're cool or something with the paparazzi taking all those pictures because of Veronica Evans. I don't understand how either one of them could score her."

The partner cop couldn't believe what he'd seen either. "Look at them sagging in their pants and strutting like gods out our precinct."

"We'll get them another time." The cop watched all three of them get into a very nice car and drive away. "You know thugs are always into something. One thing that I can say for sure, though, is that Veronica Evans is darn fine!"

Inside of Veronica Evan's car, she warned. "Don't think that we won't talk more about what happened when I get back from my Christian Women's Conference in a couple of days. You're not out of the hot water, Keyshawn. And Vern, your Rochelle said she was going to knock some sense into you when she gets back."

Vern whispered to Keyshawn, "Meow." He coughed. "You still got a problem with cat insurance?"

"What did you say, Vern?" Veronica asked. She had missed what he said. "Anyways, I cannot believe that you had me fly back here to bail you two out for acting so stupid! There's an award singing gospel singer tonight at the conference that I had better not miss on account of you two! And just because an officer pulls you over for speeding, does not give you the right to go off on them. You're the one who broke the law! I'm surprised that your old car could even go that fast, to begin with."

Vern tapped his homeboy. "Don't say shit."

"What's he talking about?"

Keyshawn answered, "He's not saying anything you did not see in the report. And you're right; I need to stop talking so much trash. But you know that I love you. That's no trash talk. So, how are you doing besides all of this mess?"

"I'm doing fine," she replied. "The conference cabins we're in do not have televisions. What I would die to watch my shows. Other than that, I got my girls with me. We're all focused."

"Sorry to hear that," said Keyshawn. He wasn't sorry. He knew the police show came on television, Wednesdays or Thursdays. It was early in the week, so she was going to miss the broadcast since she was returning Friday.

"You're a lucky mofo," said Vern, from the backseat.

18

Veronica looked at Keyshawn. "He's lucky about what?"

Keyshawn smiled, "I'm lucky because I got you, baby."

She was not just Keyshawn's girlfriend. Veronica was a famous journalist for one of the most successful, aristocratically, and fashionable celebrity magazines in the world! She was also nationally known for speaking at presidential rallies, hosting pro football games, and gracing numerous talk shows.

Therefore, paying the bail was not a financial burden for her. Her company allowed her to travel on the company jet at her every need. She had it like that. She was free to take over the world!

However, all of that freedom was going to get tested. Whenever that episode of Police Tales broadcasts, she may not watch it, but it was without doubt that she would hear about it through rumors or tabloids.

Keyshawn had been seen prior on many tabloids alongside Veronica after her split with an ex-boyfriend, a former three-time, most valuable player in professional baseball. Mr. MVP had since moved on, with his sixteen kids and sixteen baby-mommas. However, many critics believed that Veronica hadn't.

So, how did Keyshawn score a celebrity?

It all started when Keyshawn got a job at the warehouse during the time Veronica broke up with the baseball MVP. Keyshawn scanned, loaded, and delivered a package from his warehouse to her door the first time. He did it again another week, but he then broke the seal for her. Then, the third time, he blew the top off and opened it up!

Next thing he knew, Keyshawn exclusively spent a lot of time delivering empty boxes to her fancy home with his name as the sender. When they finally wore each other out in the bed, on the counter, on the couch, in the hot tub and under the house in the crawl space, the talking expanded. They dug each other's company and fell in love.

Many journalists believed Keyshawn was just the luckiest thug. He was not worth their time to write a story on. He was too dull. Everybody else figured he was just the rebound man, and he'd be leaving in a snap. Everybody in the media fantasized about her type and yet, couldn't wait to expose a so-called loser, interim boyfriend.

However, Keyshawn was indeed a good man. He worked hard and busted his ass for Veronica's heart. He was near perfection in her eyes, and she in his. Yet, he doubted himself versus the media. Now, that power had the ultimate weapon to take him down in that broadcast. It would be simple to take him down, but the episode would crush Veronica Evans as well.

It was a no-brainer that her reputation and her job were on the line after the Police Tales episode aired later in the week. Veronica was guilty by association. Therefore, it was also a no-brainer for her to break her infant-length relationship with Keyshawn. However, the heart was not so smart because sometimes, love just won't let go.

By Ashaki Boelter

Chapter 2

The Ultimatum: Him or Your Job

"**V**eronica Evans! I need to see you in my office right now!"

The entire office staff and guests of *She's Golden Magazine* stopped working. The typists paused, greeters muted, interviewed celebrities gulped, and janitors dropped their brooms. Whoever had the name Veronica must have been in some deep doo-doo because that was the boss that called her name. Whenever Ms. Cobblestone hollered for someone like that, five minutes later, they were escorted out by security without a job.

Nervously, Veronica left her cubicle and entered Ms. Cobblestone's office. The shades were drawn.

"Go on and sit down," instructed Ms. Cobblestone.

"Hello. So, Ms. Cobblestone, what's on your mind?"

"First of all, I welcome you back, Veronica. I assume you had a great time at the conference. You look so spruced up and refreshed."

"I am. I feel so renewed."

"That is wonderful. Anyways, it's time to get back to the real world! Honey, you know what's on my mind."

Gulp.

Ms. Cobblestone stood up from her desk. She refrained from further screaming, as she honestly liked Veronica, her Employee of the Year two years ago, and always a nominee. "Veronica, darling, you are a celebrity, working as a journalist here at *She's Golden*. I think back on hiring you, and quite frankly, I made you."

"What?"

"Ever since I assigned you to that interview with that hot rap artist years ago, you have been on a roll. A year after that, you found yourself interviewing the president of our country! I did that! I got you all those interviews! You have been invited to so many functions because I put you out there. I made you the celebrity you are! Your celebrity status puts dollars in my pocket. Understand? You have kept us ahead of the competition with your wonderful and intellectual interviews and insights. It doesn't make it any worse to look as good as you do either. You were the epitome of glamorous! Now, it comes to this new crap? Now, you want to burn me and the reputation of this company with a stunt like this?"

"Burn you? Huh? Wait. What are you talking about?"

"Your boyfriend is plastered all over the newsstands and on the local news channels this morning!" Ms. Cobblestone blushed. "There's even online video this morning from when you bailed your man out of jail a few days ago! Look here on my computer monitor. A weekly police show filmed the entire arrest!"

"Oh, my goodness, that's Keyshawn! I had no idea it was going to be filmed! He never told me. Are the cops holding a bag of cocaine? Oh, God! He ran for it?"

"He ran," said the boss. "That episode was on television yesterday evening during the president's speech, so over half of America saw the show!"

"I'm so sorry."

"As we all say, thank God it's Friday. You have the weekend to make your decision on dumping that loser boyfriend or coming back to work on Monday without that baggage. Am I clear?"

"You're very clear."

"Veronica, how could you do this to me? Honey, I told you from the start of getting with thugs. Look at him and look at yourself. There is no balance! If he didn't tell you about this bullshit, I could not imagine what other secrets he holds, especially when you leave town. I would hope that you're practicing safe sex because you're lined up to be nothing more than a single mother. He's a thug!"

"Honestly, he's not that bad. He's not *that* thuggish. All of this press has got to be a mistake."

Ms. Cobblestone slammed a brand new copy of another celebrity magazine on her desk, which was also released this morning.

Veronica gulped.

"The mail clerk brought this to my attention this morning," said Ms. Cobblestone. "Then I fired him, of course, because he brought a competitor's magazine into my office. Anyways, the front cover shows not only your boyfriend holding your hand, but his other hand is cupping his nuts. His friend's back is turned to the camera, and clearly, his pants are sagging where the world can see his booty-bite and his off-colored stain."

"I assure you that both of these guys are not that bad."

"Look at the picture! Someone does not belong there!"

Veronica knew it was wise to simply listen.

"Honey, this kind of publicity is going to slow your roll around here. Do you understand that? Veronica, I've already received eight canceled appointments of yours this morning."

"Ms. Cobblestone, I am so sorry. I'll make it up to you!"

"You bet your ass that you're sorry, and you'll make it up."

23

"What can I do to gain your trust back?"

"I have an idea," answered Ms. Cobblestone. "After you dump that thug, get back to the ex-boyfriend. That would also make great headlines."

"What?"

"Veronica, do not look at me like that! The entire world thinks you should have tried harder with Edmund 'The Home-run Gun' Rasmussen. He was a real man, a highly profiled professional athlete! He was last year's MVP, for heaven's sake!"

"I do not appreciate what you are saying, you know. I'm not going to allow this company to whore me out!"

"I don't pay you to appreciate what I have to say," replied Ms. Cobblestone. "You know what kind of business you do. We do upper-class celebrity interviews because we are upper-class journalists! Do you think your interviewees are going to take you seriously after knowing about you clowning around in life with gangsters on your off-hours? Get some class back, go home, and dump the thug."

"I cannot believe that you're making me pick between my job and my man. I'm one of the greatest journalists you've ever had!"

"Am I stuttering in here?" Ms. Cobblestone angrily stood over Veronica. "You need to get your priorities straight! You didn't come in here with that thug when I hired you. That's all I hear about when it comes to you these days in the office."

"My business is none of this company's business."

"Well," explained Ms. Cobblestone, "you are the one that walks around the office, blabbing all of your business here. Do you think gossip stops with the person you're talking to around here? She's Golden magazine is a gossip company! Hello? Nobody holds a secret in this building, child. I know everything. For example, I know that your thug boyfriend loves to suck on your toes for foreplay!"

"Wait! Hold on! What?"

"Well, that's not all I know, either."

"Excuse me? Stop right there. I don't believe this!"

24

By Ashaki Boelter

"Believe it, honey," said Ms. Cobblestone. "I'm not here to burst your bubble. I have a boss, just like you have one—his reputation matters to me. Veronica, you know that I don't want you to go, and that's why you're still employed this morning. I'm the only one who fought to keep you aboard! Now protect my ass by dropping the loser this weekend."

Veronica's parents were workaholics that put their jobs in front of their relationship, and that caused a divorce. Yet, both of her parents are now successful after their split. With that in mind, Veronica valued her job, so she agreed with her boss.

"Just start over," said Ms. Cobblestone. "That's it. Take a deep breath and understand that there are a lot of men out there in the world that would represent you better than some crotch-tugging thug. I'm sure it was nothing more than a sexual rebound anyways between the two of you. If you want a relationship, you're just going to have to be more patient. A real man will show up at your door someday, cute, packing, and successful."

Veronica sniffed and then wiped away her tears. "Ms. Cobblestone, maybe you're right."

"I am right." Mr. Cobblestone adjusted her blouse. She winked. "You have to move on with your wonderful life. While you take care of your personal life, I did help you with one thing earlier. I've scheduled you great interviews for redemption. I'll give you details at a later time. For now, I want you to take the rest of the day off. Use the weekend to better yourself. If you need a week, I can give you that. I know how hard breaking up is to do, especially when sometimes, love won't let go."

"Okay."

"When you come back to work, I want the real Veronica Evans! I truly have your back. Oh, I have a downloaded copy of that police episode on this disk. I know that you haven't seen it because if you had, you would've called in sick today."

"Thank you, Ms. Cobblestone," said Veronica. She dabbed away her tears, took a deep breath, and reached for the door. "I'll take care of things, I promise. Thanks for being there for me."

Veronica marched out of her boss's office. She walked into the company cafeteria and began to pour herself a cup of coffee.

"Are you alright?" Devon Hamilton, a co-worker and suave friend that she admired for his journalism about adopting children from Africa, a co-worker, sat at a nearby table. He had been an employee at She's Golden for as long as she had. Devon realistically knew a lot more about her than her boyfriend, as she spent, just like most Americans, most of her life at work.

"Keyshawn just doesn't get it!"

"You don't have to tell me, Veronica. I saw the show last night. Hey, welcome back, though. How was the church conference?"

"Devon, I don't know what's gotten into Keyshawn as of late." Veronica took a sip of her coffee. "I know Keyshawn is working a lot more hours around those thugs at his warehouse job, but I think he's going in a direction that I'm not caring for because of it. After work, he's been hanging out more with thugs. And I told him that he doesn't have to work as much, but he's about making more money than me. Until Keyshawn makes more, he feels like he's less of a man."

"And we all know that won't happen in a million years," stated Devon. "How can he compete financially with the great Veronica Evans? I guess that Keyshawn will always feel like a little gangster boy. Yet, I think that I know how he feels. I make less than everybody around here and cannot buy a date! However, if only women in this company knew that my late father, a world explorer, left me with a huge inheritance to live on and great friends, whom I grew up with, from all around the world."

"That is so awesome, Devon. You have a lot to brag about."

"Uh, well. Uh, golly gee," Devon quickly changed the subject, to not sound anymore like a privileged prick. "Listen, Veronica, most of us could hear Ms. Cobblestone through the thin walls when she was talking to you. I was wondering if there is anything I could do."

"No. I'm sure there isn't, but thanks."

"Not really," replied Devon. "I only want to protect my friend. You're like my best friend around here."

"Thanks. You're like my best friend too."

Devon admired that. "So listen. Some of my inherited

investments include treasures in Egypt. Well, I've since made great friendships with some folks out that way. I can, if you want, help your reputation by setting you up with an interview with my friend, the great King Abu Jiffy Tutu Gumbo."

"Get out of here! Do you personally know King Abu Jiffy Tutu Gumbo, the Egyptian ambassador?"

"We hang out from time to time. King Gumbo will be in Spain for a conference. I could arrange, for you, an exclusive interview with him in a heartbeat. Your appointment book cannot look all that promising after the stunt your boyfriend pulled on Police Tales."

"Oh, I'm down! I owe you big time!"

"I'll make it happen in a few weeks. You are a good reporter, and I know that you deserve a shot at continuing to be the best in the world. I love your work!"

"You are so sweet!"

Devon was ready to rip Veronica's clothes off and hump her in the work pantry, but he was classically working a classy woman. He had to keep calm for now. He calculated things were just too hot at the time to jump, and his complete plan to score with her could backfire.

Veronica hugged him to his surprise. Devon nearly broke his back not to make pelvic contact, as she would've known his dirty little secret: He wanted to hit it three or four times yesterday.

She patted his back, turned away, and walked down the hallway towards the elevator at the end of the hall.

"What are you looking at?" asked Hugo. He was an editor at She's Golden and more so Devon's real best friend. "Put your tongue back into your mouth, soldier. She's not ready."

"What?"

"I saw you staring at her ass! Yeah, man, you know you want it like the rest of the guys around here! I have caught a glance so many times when she walks by my desk that I excuse myself five to ten times a day to the men's john! You cannot find a behind like that in any national publication! She is oblivious to her blessings."

"Yes, she is." Devon licked his lips. "Yet, some little thug gets to hit that at home. That is an injustice to humanity!"

"Well, hold on now. From the walls of Ms. Cobblestone's office this morning, Veronica may be ending her thug relationship as soon as she gets home."

"She's going to need a hug, eventually."

"Look, you need to get some of that!" Hugo pulled a comb out and combed his slick hair back. "I know you dig her. The other day on the golf course, we were talking about whom we'd hit up from work. Remember? Well, now, you have a chance if you play your cards right. Even if she gets back with him, now is your time to be the cleanup man; get her while she's on the rebound! It won't mean anything because she's vulnerable, and everyone knows we do stupid things in those times, so there's no shame in the game."

"You think so? Should I go on and hit it? She's been such a good friend. I don't want to ruin that!"

"Seriously, are you a man? She's vulnerable right now! She trusts you! She breaks up; you hit it. It's that simple."

"Yeah, she does trust me."

"You're already in her emotions! Most guys around here see her and wonder how to get closer to her. Look, just take her out for a drink and get her a little tipsy! I bet she's a freak if she likes thugs."

"Hold on. Veronica is coming back this way! Be quiet."

"Hi, Hugo," greeted Veronica.

"Hello, Veronica, how are you doing?"

"Don't ask."

"I won't."

Veronica noticed the sweat rolling from Hugo and Devon's foreheads. "What are you guys whispering about? Are there any more rumors or surprises that I should be aware of?"

"What rumors? We're just talking fantasy football secrets. You know how we are about fantasy football."

The two men walked away to the cafeteria and sat down.

Veronica followed them into the cafeteria and walked over to the sink to wash out her coffee mug before leaving for the day. She pulled a napkin out of the dispenser to then dry it. Oops! She dropped that napkin on the floor, and then she slowly bent over to pick it up. She knocked over somebody's bowl of peanuts.

"Why would somebody leave their food on the edge of the sink?" She scrambled to pick up the scattered nuts.

"Oh my god, dude, I would…. Wow! Would you look at all that booty?" Hugo nudged Devon. "I'd like to hit that all night long!"

"You're telling me, my friend!"

"Devon, have you ever simply tried to slip her some cash or something? You never know! She could be a closet hooker!"

"Come on." Devon chuckled.

"Quick! Get a picture on your cell phone! Then text me back a picture of that! My battery just died. Hurry up, Devon!"

"Where did I leave my cell phone?"

"No really though, what are you guys so excited about?" Veronica asked. She stood up, turned around, and walked over to share in the good-spirited conversation. She was unaware. "I could use a good laugh, guys."

Veronica never thought of herself as a man magnet, nor did she believe that upscale folks with degrees from prominent colleges and mature attitudes could carry sick perversions. She was oblivious to the two perverts' ill behavior.

"We were just discussing *how much cash* the government *stiffs* are putting *into* the *deep spac*e program." Hugo didn't even make eye contact with her eyes.

"Ooh... Politics are not my thing. Well, I had better get out of here. I have some personal issues to attend to."

"Take care," said Devon. "Remember what I said. I'll be there if you need anything. Okay?"

"Thanks," she replied and walked away.

"It's only a matter of time," said Hugo. "I saw the way she looked at you, Devon. You really should just ask her out!"

"Hugo, the last thing I want is for her ex-boyfriend coming after me. He's probably territorial; I sure would be if I had Veronica! Besides, I do not want to be a rebound man for a woman like her. I want a woman like her forever! See, I need somebody else to break that ice before I climb that icy mound."

"That's smart," Hugo claimed. "So then, you can use me! I'd like to be the one to break the ice and climb!"

"Come on, Hugo. Let's be intelligent about this."

"I'm not that bad looking, Devon. Come on!"

"Look. I have an idea already." Devon completely ignored his friend's assessment of himself. "I know somebody that can have any woman he wants. He's the king of players: King Abu Jiffy Tutu Gumbo. From my dealings with him, I know that all of his wives are super happy! He's skillful when it comes to convincing women to sleep with him. No woman can resist his charm. So, not only did I send Veronica to get a good story, I sent her his way to get screwed."

"So, Veronica won't be returning to work?"

"No, you idiot. Veronica is so career-minded, she'll return. But when she returns, she'll have gotten over Keyshawn after being with the King Gumbo. That would make the king, the rebound. After women get over that hump, they become available to any man with no ex-boyfriend strings attached!"

Chapter 3

You Were Never Qualified

She disappointingly smacked her lips, turned the television off, and carelessly tossed the remote control over to the other couch. Veronica had just watched the police episode on the burned disk her boss gave her earlier. It was still early in the morning, as she listened for Keyshawn to awaken. He usually worked nights. He often woke up about *now*.

"Oh Keyshawn," called Veronica, "please come out here? I would like to ask you about something."

"Good morning, baby. Did you take the day off or something? Let me take a whiz right quick, and then I'll be right there."

Keyshawn detoured to the bathroom and patiently stood there and punished the porcelain. He knew that the swan call she gave him a minute ago was a smokescreen to get him in the room with her to discuss something terrible. She was never home in the mornings, either. Yet, he kept a positive spin to his confusion.

Maybe she came back home for a quickie? After all, it'd been a week since they got busy, and last night when she returned home, Keyshawn was already asleep. That's why this morning, he brushed his grill, greased, and forked his Afro out. He threw on some cologne.

"Good morning," greeted Keyshawn as he strutted out to the living room. "I am so glad you're back."

Veronica looked him dead in the eye. "What you did last weekend was horrible, and you hurt a lot of people."

"I'm sorry. Let's go into the bedroom and make it *all* better!"

"I can lose my job over this thing, Keyshawn!"

"Hey! Who loves you, babe? Chill out."

"You need to listen," answered Veronica. "My boss wants me to dump you if I want to continue working for the best-selling magazine company in the nation! Your situation indirectly affected the reputation of my company. I'm so finished! You know that I've already gone through tabloid hell with my ex!"

"Let them write! Everybody knows that your ex was a dog. There's no comparison. I treat you well, and you know that. So they got me on that police show, which is fabricated. We didn't have drugs on us, we weren't drinking, and that wasn't either one of us running from the cops. Veronica, it was all scripted. It was a show!"

"They're already printing up that you're not any different than my ex." Veronica shook her head. "Except this time, they're printing stories about how you didn't finish college and that you are simply my boy toy because I'm on the rebound! Supposedly, I've been made out to have a thug fetish! Look, Keyshawn, I think I need some space."

"Are you for real? Come on, baby. You know that I love you and you love me. We know what's up, baby! Let them print lies. What matters is that I told you the truth and that you trust me. Do not let other people determine our love. Our shit is about you and me!"

"You're not drinking and driving, sniffing that shit?"

"Baby, come on! You know me!"

"Why do you still hang out with Vern?" Veronica never trusted Vern, as his lifestyle was a counseling nightmare. "You're always going to be guilty by association with him! Therefore, that makes *me* guilty by association with you!"

"Come again? You do know that you cannot believe everything you see on television?"

"Do I look like I'm five years old? Of course, I'm not going to believe everything! I know that I saw two thugs misbehaving."

"What was shown was partly me, and the other part was a stunt man," explained Keyshawn. "All I did was speed, and the cop pulled me over. I was in the wrong place, speeding at the wrong time. The alcohol and cocaine weren't mines! You've got to believe me; I'm innocent! All of that show was phony!"

"I bailed you out of *real* jail, Keyshawn! I signed real documents, and I paid a hefty amount of real money!"

"I know, baby. I know."

"I want you to stay the hell away from that dirty bastard, a so-called friend of yours if you want to keep me."

Keyshawn shook his head. "You're asking me to give up my best friend? Can I at least have one friend of my own? I mean… Damn! He's been my best friend since kindergarten! You want me to give him up for what, your stuck-up, yuppie friends and lies?"

"Excuse me? My friends are not stuck-up or yuppie!"

"Just because you're so high and mighty around all those rich white folks doesn't automatically make a black man a criminal!"

"Well then... prove it! You're the one who went to jail!"

"I'm innocent of what the world is trying to make of me!"

"Keyshawn, the world is full of black doctors and counselors and pastors and smart folks," explained Veronica. "I know because I interview a lot of these intellectuals. These successful black folks are what also make the world go round. They know how it works. As far as they are concerned, you are a criminal! How's the saying go? If it walks and talks like a duck, it's got to be!"

"What in the hell has gotten into your black ass? You're either going to believe I am who I say I am or you're not!"

"Okay, Keyshawn, who are you?"

"Are you being for real?"

"The facts are already out there on the table," replied Veronica. "Maybe you were just my rebound? You still hang with thugs. I mean, you've cheated on me before, so it's not like you're anything better than any kind of thug I've ever imagined. You're all the same."

"That cheating thing, you claim, was at the beginning when we first started having sex. That shouldn't even count as cheating! I hadn't asked you out yet! I barely even knew you."

Veronica exhaled. "I am one of the world's greatest journalists, and I think it's time for you to pack up your stuff and get the hell on! You can't be trusted, man. Boy, bye!"

"Get your palm out of my face! Don't do this, Veronica!"

"I do not want to hear all of that whining from any man. It's not attractive. Go, please!"

Keyshawn was crushed. He blurted, "I'm not an animal! Talk at me like I'm a man! That's what I am! I'm a man! Understand?"

"Man, don't you raise your voice at me in my damn house!" Veronica shook her head. "You know Keyshawn, my boss was right. My career came first! No man should take that away from a woman if they love her. You nearly got me fired with the stunt you pulled with the police. You are so inconsiderate and... *and* stupid!"

"Is that right? Well, your boss can suck my dick!"

"See, that's what I'm talking about." Veronica pointed to Keyshawn as he held his balls. "Why must you grab your stuff when you're uptight about something like some gangster thug? You're not even in my league, Keyshawn. I've been blind for months! My boss, the news critics, my friends, my family, my pastor, and all of my co-workers were right. You know what?"

"What?"

"I'd never give up my career *for someone like you* to only end up somewhere *on welfare*, barefoot in the kitchen, *battered*, abused, and with *nine hundred kids* in a three hundred square foot *shack*."

"Veronica! Hell to the Nah' you didn't just say all that!"

"I said for you to not raise your voice at me in my house!"

"What? You're yelling! But you know what? Fuck everybody, you know, all those punk-ass suckers!"

Veronica jumped to another level for the icing on the cake. "The more I think about it, Keyshawn, I realize that even God wants us to break up. That explains the spiritual strength I was building up last week at the conference. All week long, I was trying to figure out why God was strengthening my heart. It turns out that finding the strength to leave your tired ass was what the conference was all about. Dear Lord, Jesus Christ, thank you for saving me from growing old with this idiot!"

"What? Fuck this shit. I'm out!"

"Thank God," replied Veronica. "I'm going out for a bit myself. When I return, I expect you and all of your cheap ass garbage to be gone. Don't think I won't bring the cops back up in here either to put a restraining order on you. After seeing you on that TV show, I'm sure they would love to revisit you."

"Fuck you, Veronica! Fuck you!"

"Fuck you, Keyshawn!"

"Fuck you!"

"Hurry up and get your shit out of my house!" Veronica stormed out the front door with her palm up in the air, got into her car, and skidded out the driveway. She flew down the street like a rocket.

"Damn! I can't believe what just happened." Keyshawn stood there, raged, and hurt. He picked up his cell phone and called Vern.

"What's up, Keyshawn?"

"Veronica kicked me out," answered Keyshawn. "She saw the police show. She doesn't want me anymore, Vern. It's over."

"Man, I' m sorry. Know what I'm saying?"

"Fuck her. I need a spot to kick it."

"Come over. You know you can camp out on my sofa."

"Thanks."

"You'll be alright." Vern felt terrible for his friend. "You know that the cop show was only a part of why she put you out. Know what I'm saying? She's been trying to find a reason, I'd bet, for months. You and I know what it's *really* about. It's about that cheating you had done when you two were meeting for the first time. I told you not to tell her about that!"

"I wasn't with either gal at the time, man. How is she going to claim me before I asked her out? I said hello to her that day I dropped off a package, went to a party that night and hit up that nasty chick, and the next day, I delivered another package to Veronica's house. That's when I started talking to her. She went back and paid for an investigator to track my whereabouts before we dated."

"She's thorough."

"Man, this has nothing to do with that. It has to do with her stupid job, the cop show, and her reputation!"

"You know, maybe you're right? You've been the perfect gentleman, as far as I know. She broke up with that baseball player before you, so maybe you were just a rebound guy. Maybe you were never her type, and she was never over the ex."

"I don't need to hear any of that right now."

"I don't mean to sound harsh, but she used you to get over her ex. You were just a fuck rebound. Know what I'm saying?"

"Come on, man! You're killing me."

"You were never qualified for Veronica, bro! Just accept your loss and move on to another ho. Know what I'm saying? Don't spend the rest of your life trying to prove anything to her. Amputate!"

"Like, cut it off?"

"Yeah, cut that shit off! Now, hurry up and pack; you get the hell out of there. Tonight, I'm taking you to the club! I heard that a few hot celebs would be in there, including the news weather chick, Grand Camorra."

"My pastor, the last time I went to church last summer, said that God could fix all things. Veronica came back from the Christian conference and dumped me! When is the Lord going to help me? If he can't help me, I wish He would just end my misery."

Chapter 4

Somebody Needs a Hug

After a few days of dodging and deleting Keyshawn's obnoxious and overly sympathetic apologies on her voicemail, Veronica simply got a new number.

However, her new voicemail ended up with plenty of messages too. They weren't from Keyshawn. Veronica had become one of the most sought after celebrities in the media, thanks to Keyshawn. Her closest associates took their share of money to give her number away to various gossip journalists of the industry.

Although Veronica was now labeled a hoodlum and whore throughout conservative media and outlets, she was not going to lose focus. She planned to let her actions speak for her and wanted to give the biggest and best interview in the world.

She had an interview scheduled this morning with King Abu Jiffy Tutu Gumbo, the Egyptian ambassador. Initially, the meeting was planned to occur in Spain, but the king already planned to attend a significant pro wrestling event in New York, the same week. Most celebrities stayed at this particular motel. So, he agreed to an interview at his luxurious hotel suite.

After Veronica's plane landed in New York, she dashed to her nearby hotel and freshened up. Then she left for King Gumbo's suite, along with assigned camera operators, to interview him.

Outside of her wildest dreams, accompanied by several security officers, the great King Abu Jiffy Tutu Gumbo walked into the room. He wore a white linen robe, lined with goat hair, and decorated with beads, gold jewelry, and feathers. A crown atop his head sat pleasantly on his long hair, which came down his face into a perfectly trimmed beard. He sat down, adjusted his kilt, and greeted the cameramen and the host, Veronica Evans. The security guards left the room to guard the door. It was time to start the interview.

"Mr. King Abu Jiffy Tutu Gumbo, it is a privilege for me to be sitting here interviewing you today," stated Veronica. She was going to get paid big bucks to do the interview, not only by the company she worked for but by the king himself. She couldn't be more privileged to be able to talk to him one on one, as he sorely granted interviews.

"Eh… It is my pleasure to have you sitting with me. Yes?"

"For those viewers watching this interview, who may not know you, it is important for them to know that you have been King of Canon, Egypt for over twenty years. You have been recently nominated for the Nobel Peace Prize for your wonderful book of poetry, and you have a lucrative movie offer from Hollywood. That's part of why you're here, as producers are in town for the pro wrestling event. I even here there is a movie being filmed here also. On top of that, you just signed a two-year contract to be the spokesperson for an airline."

"Yes… yes… It is Global Wide Airlines. I knew I could trust you for having your facts together. I am delighted to do this interview with somebody who is intellectual and sexy."

"You have a full plate," said Veronica. She smiled at the king, but he wouldn't make eye contact with her.

"Yes." The king replied, but he fantasized about how he wanted to position Veronica in his bed across the room and make love after the interview! "You can get on with the interview."

"So King Gumbo, what is next to come for the hardest working king in the world? King, did you understand my question? Hello?"

"What's next? I want to spend the night with you, Veronica!"

"King, that's charming. However, we need to conduct this interview in a way for the world to watch and learn from."

"We stop the interview now to make whoopee!" He sat against Veronica, placed his arm around her shoulder, and licked her neck like a lollipop! *Slurp! Slurp! Slurp! Slurp! Slurp!* "Ah... yeah..."

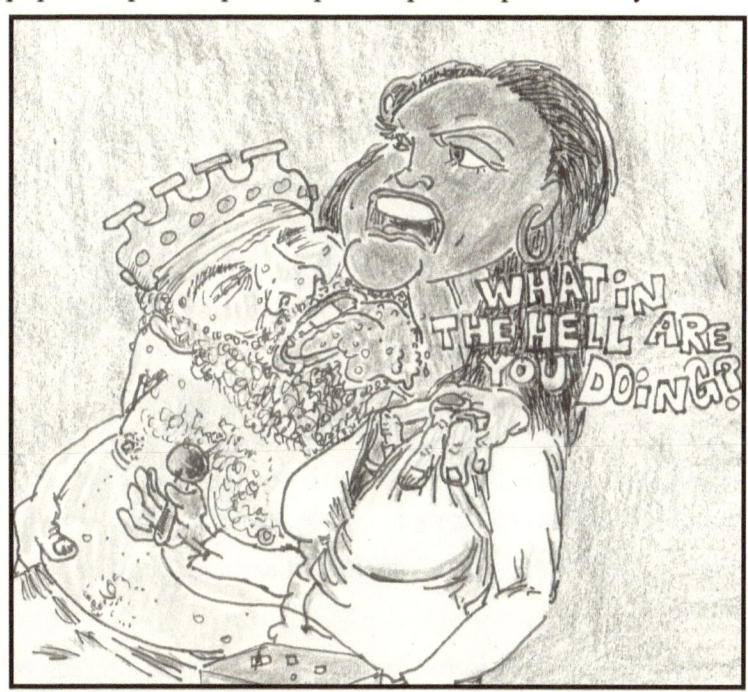

"What in the hell are you doing?" Veronica was angry! She shoved the king and stepped back. "Yuck! You disgusting pig!"

The king slowly stood up and then dropped his cloth! "I make love to you now. Yes? We make baby now!"

"We're doing an interview here, you moron! Put your clothes

back on, and let's be professional. I'll end this interview, otherwise!"

"The interview is done then, tramp!" King Tutu snapped his fingers and pointed to the door. The camera crew obeyed and instantly left the room! Veronica didn't know the network production crew, which Devon hired, at all.

"You guys cannot leave me alone with this jerk!" shouted Veronica. "You guys get back in here right now!"

"Ha! They're not coming back! I am the king!"

"If you lay one hand on me again, I'll scream!"

The king stood in front of the door. "Veronica, let's just listen to reason. I know that you date athletes for their money, which I have. You date thugs because you like it rough. I will make a deal. You're single now. If you give me what I want, I swear that I will give you the interview of your career. Just take off your fancy clothes and let me show you real, athletic thug passion. You get on my bed, you scrumptious skank! Show me your breasts! I want to tear you up!"

Veronica screamed her head off!

"Go on and scream." King Tutu laughed. "I reserved the entire floor above me, below me, and the floor we're on. Nobody can hear you. It's helpless. Now, bring that black ass to me!"

"You take your hands off of me!"

The king grabbed her arm, tossed her across the room, and high jumped the bed she rolled over! Unfortunately, he crashed against the wall and slid down it because Veronica moved away just in time. She dashed for the door, but tripped over a pair of the king's sandals!

"Now, I've got you!" declared the king. He climbed upon her.

"No!"

"No means *yes* in my kingdom!" The king aggressively felt her up and maneuvered his hips upon her. "You got what I like! I took three blue pills an hour ago, so this should be satisfying!"

"Get off of me!" Veronica felt the king's ashy fingers caress her bare skin underneath her slip! She wouldn't give in. "I don't care if you're a king! You're about to get your royal ass kicked!"

"I want to make a baby right now, Veronica!"

"I said to get off of me!" shouted Veronica. She rolled the king over, angrily cocked her fist, and threw a rocket uppercut into the king's lumpy nuts!

Whud!

"Ooh! Hoot-hoot! Ooh!" cried the king. He felt for his balls, but one was missing. "You son of a bitch, I can't find one of my nuts! Where is it? Where is my nut? I cannot feel it!"

"I warned you that I wasn't playing when I said *no*, you bastard! You wanted to take advantage of me?"

As the disgruntled king hunched over in pain, Veronica grabbed him by his lumpy nut and hurriedly walked his stumbling ass into the bathroom. That's where she slam-dunked his nut sack in the toilet and slammed the molded toilet seat down onto his arched back! She then stomped her foot down against that seat and flushed the toilet. The blue chemicals in the toilet water sizzled and burned the king's pubic hairs off!

"You had better not disrespect me again, asshole! Do you hear me, king? Huh? You let that be a lesson to you!"

"You witch!" screamed the king. "Get out of my room and leave me alone! Please, I beg of you! Leave! And tell Devon to go and hump a diseased camel for sending your sorry ass here! You're stupid! I'll never talk to him again!"

"Oh yes, *Devon*."

"Tell him that I never want to hear from him again! He said that you were easy, but you're just a stingy, little whore! Get out!"

"Goodbye, king."

The king threw a shoe at the door after Veronica walked out.

She angrily marched down the hotel hallway and promised that she was going to kill Devon when she returned to the office place. She rode the elevator down to the lobby.

"Veronica, how did the interview go?" asked the hotel manager at the front desk. "That king is the greatest man I've ever met. That was a short interview, though. You were only here for less than thirty minutes. Was everything good?"

Veronica looked over at the king's security and Devon's assigned camera guys, who sat in the lobby, eating burgers and fries, reading magazines, and playing cards. She popped her knuckles.

"Ma'am, are you okay?"

"Can you just please get me a cab before I go crazy in here?" Veronica looked out the front windows of the hotel. "There doesn't seem to be one out there. Pick up the phone now!"

"Yes, ma'am!" The hotel manager picked up the phone receiver and dialed away.

That's when a warm rush of air shot up the back of her neck hairs. The settled voice asked, "Are you the lovely Veronica Evans?"

Veronica had a headache and wasn't in the mood for flirtations from any more egotistical dimwits. She didn't even turn to see who was breathing up her neck.

"Not now."

"Hello? I'm Carl. I don't believe we've ever met, but the pleasure is all mines. I love your journalism."

"Beat it before I call the cops, mister."

"Wow," mumbled Carl. "I haven't heard a response like that since high school. Lady, tell me. Is it my breath or the sound of my voice that annoys you? Or are you having a bad day?"

"Why are men so conceited?" asked Veronica. She angrily turned around with her finger pointed, ready to tell the man off. However, she suddenly put a halt to that lousy business.

"Can we start again? Please?"

Veronica turned around so fast that if she had her fist out, she would have knocked out the heavyweight champion of the world with one hit! She was going to light the man up with an insult.

"Oh my Lord, Jesus, you're Carl Cleveland!" Veronica gulped. She was no longer angry; she was embarrassed! "I am so sorry! If I had known it was you, I would've greeted you better."

The six-three, beautiful, milk chocolate Hollywood hunk in front of her, melted her into her red pumps. If there were ever a man she could marry without knowing him before, it would've been him.

44

By Ashaki Boelter

Carl Cleveland had been in the television and the movie industry since he was a teenager. With a few great films and sexy spreads across many hunk magazines throughout the last twenty years, there wasn't a woman alive, married or not, young or old, who could resist his unique charm and distinct beauty.

It was widely rumored that Carl visited a high school last year to speak at a graduation ceremony, and it was postponed to the following day because all the females fainted for the night. Worse yet, it was rumored a few years ago that he had visited one of his elderly relatives in a convalescent home, and the moment he got there, all the female senior citizens stroked out and died, all holding a pair of their panties to give to him. Carl was one of the hottest Hollywood actors ever to grace the planet, and there he stood in front of Veronica.

Minutes too soon, a yellow cab rolled up to the hotel doors. Veronica couldn't get a word out of her mouth, as Carl rearranged his schedule with another front desk attendant.

"It appears that my cab has arrived," said Veronica.

"That's great," replied Carl. He hesitated to articulate his sprung feelings. "I saw you look at the gentlemen over there and roll your eyes. Is everything okay? You're not in any trouble with them, are you? Do you need me to do something about it? I have bodyguards near that would knock their blocks off."

"No, I don't think I need help, but thanks for asking. I have to leave now. My ride is waiting."

Carl saw an exceptional radiance of beauty in Veronica, even if the raindrops outside the windows drew a soggy frame around her. He ran out of the hotel doors and hailed her. "Wait! Veronica, do you have a little time right now for maybe a cup of coffee down the block? I passed by an elegant little diner not too far from here. Maybe I can entertain you about the new film I'm working on out here in New York? We can call it an impromptu interview if you want for your magazine. You'll be getting first tabs about the new film I'm working on out here in New York."

"Wouldn't you get swamped by fans out there in public? You're a top of the line actor and all."

"My driver is my bodyguard and not to mention, my cousin. I've seen him karate chop a bear's head off! He's got an eye out on everything. With my entourage, I'm sure we'll be okay. I promise."

"Well, I have no plans right now." Veronica slid her hand underneath her damp bangs and moved her hair behind her ear. Then she smiled. "Sure. Why not? Carl, I could use a cup of coffee."

"Splendid. Come on, right this way."

The reserved cab driver drove away. "Screw you jerks!"

Carl kindly escorted Veronica to his enormous black limousine, which was parked in front of the taxi before it left. On the way to the café, he talked about his new movie called *Double Chocolate, Pour It On,* and how he had performed twelve soft sex scenes throughout his career with other cute actresses. He was excited about working this time around with a Hollywood icon, the beautiful Shirley Love. She was his teenage obsession and now, old as dirt.

"Well, it's not like you're doing anything for real," said Veronica. "It's only acting. Right, Carl? It is only acting, right?"

"Why, of course." Carl quickly changed the subject. "So, are you doing alright since the breakup? I don't want to pry, and I don't want to ever get in the way of unfinished business between couples. Not to say that I'm hitting on you. We've all heard, you know."

Veronica looked at Carl's perfect eyes. "I'm managing."

"I lost my woman a year ago, and I'm just getting over that," said Carl. "We were together for over ten years too long!"

The first thing Veronica thought was that Carl cheated.

"No," said Carl. "I can hear you thinking out loud. I didn't cheat on her. She left me because she didn't want to lie to herself anymore. She realized that she was only interested in women at some point. I loved that woman. She was so good for me."

"Well, at least she was good and honest with you." Veronica was still upset with Keyshawn and hadn't talked to anybody about it until now. "My ex was such a jerk. He lied about drinking and doing drugs. He hung out with the worst kind of guys. Then he goes and publicly humiliates himself on national television. I think I have worked hard and long enough to reap benefits to find a good man, one that lives a common-sense life. You know?"

"You do deserve that, but there is no perfect man."

"Okay, that's fair. However, there are better men."

"I read the article about what happened on the police show," said Carl. "Some of it is true, but I'd bet some of it is also false. Some of those reality cop shows are phony."

"Carl, *he has* also cheated on me."

"That would be the icing," said Carl. He ordered his cousin to drive around the city before going to the café. The backseat conversation was much too personal for walking around the public and possibly Paparazzi.

"It was when we first got together," said Veronica. She wiped away her tears. "However, once it was done, I just haven't been able to trust him. I didn't know how to get past that. Then he had to go and get arrested! His issues were going to not only drive me to my grave, but I could have lost my job over his shit!"

"You wouldn't be so broken up if you didn't love him," replied

Carl. "It eats at me to see folks broken up with things that can be fixed with time and God upstairs. Have you ever tried to go to church for encouragement and healing?"

"I didn't know you were a faith-based man."

"Yep, I am mostly on Easter and Christmas!"

"At least you are honest; you're so funny."

"What about revenge?" Carl wasn't blind. Veronica was hot.

"I won't ever stoop to that level. Out of all the scandalous celebrity stories I've covered, revenge is making a game out of problems. The game is nothing but shame in the end. Like I said in other words, I don't have times to play games with my life."

"Well, that's good," said Carl. "You're incredibly sharp. Maybe you were just too good for him? Wow. All this talk takes me back to my ex and brings me down a little. I don't know if I ever got over that woman. *Sometimes, love just won't let go*, I guess."

"It sounds like somebody needs a hug. Come here, Carl."

Veronica lustfully leaned over to her favorite male actor and got all up in his muscular business. She once hugged her television at home before with him on the screen, but to feel every abdominal muscle, his warmth, and his firm pectorals against her stiffness, was exciting! To Veronica, he smelled so sensational with a bit of spice and vanilla, while his moaning created a drop or two. All of her problems and Keyshawn became a distant memory.

Chapter 5

Getting out of Carl Cleveland's Car!

"Come on! Keyshawn, you cannot just sit on your ass all day, expecting a bitch to come back. Know what I'm saying?"

"She knows how I'd be if things got as they did," muttered Keyshawn. He was all torn up inside, while his breath stank and he cried away his trickling eye boogers. "Why hasn't she called me on my cell or something? Not even a text… Do you not get any reception in this house? Go and check your phone! Maybe she reached yours? She could've texted!"

"You need to chill," said Vern. "I can see that after five days, you can't just let go of her. I get it. Know what I'm saying? I'm not trying to be a punk-ass friend, but I have got a glimpse of Veronica's booty too. I wouldn't be able to let her go so easily, either. If you

49

want to go and get her back, I guess that I support you. Know what I'm saying? You get the hell off of my couch, and let's go get her!"

Keyshawn was psyched. However, he couldn't get up. After constipation for five days and laziness, he was glued by the funk into the couch pillows. He hadn't changed his draws in the five days!

"Man, you need to get your dirty behind off of my couch!"

"She's not off of work until the evening."

"Well, then we will head to her job while she's working," advised Vern. "If she's the one you want, are you going to let some job get in the way? You need to be a man, bro!"

"I don't know about this. What if Veronica's friends get involved? What if she gets agitated? I could cause her to lose her job if it gets out of hand."

"What? If her friends get all up in the business, telling her that she should dump you when they don't even know you, you can put a lid on that mess by facing them all! Know what I'm saying?"

"I'll take them all on!"

"That's right! Show them who you are! It's a gossip company, so leave them something to gossip about: Your love!"

"Yeah, you're right! I'll show them!"

"So Keyshawn, go on and find my beige suit in my closet. That's my player suit! Take a good shower. Then, we're going to the car dealership. We will test drive a brand new car up to her job. That way, we look like we're high rollers. Know what I'm saying?"

"Yeah, boy, I got it! Wait. Why can't I just drive my car?"

"Dude, please. And make sure that you grab some roses from my neighbor's bushes before we head down there."

A bit later, around the lunch hour, Keyshawn drove up to the front of the She's Golden magazine company in a brand new car with his homeboy. They had pulled off all the sales stickers from the windows and put in a soulful, burned CD of music. The salesman that rode with them was a friend, and he was dropped off at home.

"Forever, my lady!" declared Vern. "Know what I'm saying?"

"They must have a big-time celebrity up in there for an interview," declared Keyshawn. He pulled the brand new car up to the main doors and parked behind the longest limousine he had ever seen in his life!

"That is a big ass car, dude."

"Look at the size of that bodyguard standing outside the car! You know that he's juiced up on something! Damn."

"I wouldn't want to mess with him. Know what I'm saying?"

"Well… Here I go. I'm going to march right into that company and… Well, I'm not leaving here without my woman!"

"Go get your gal! Yeah! Do your thing, Keyshawn!"

Keyshawn opened his door and placed his foot onto the sidewalk. "Vern, it looks like the celebrity is getting out of the limo. Quick! Pass me a pen and paper so I can get an autograph just in case it's a huge star! Hurry up!"

"Find your own, homeboy!" Vern already stood outside of the car; he was ready to ask for an autograph.

"That's Carl Cleveland!" Keyshawn was star struck. Carl Cleveland movies served as a player dictionary to many soulful guys, dating back since the black cinematic rush of action hero movie days in the nineteen-seventies! "My man, Casanova Carl, is in the house!"

Carl had been copied and imitated for years but never duplicated when it came to romancing women and being super cool. Carl was known to write his phrases for the movies he starred in, too; those lines worked for most players today in the clubs.

Vern credited Carl Cleveland for helping his ugly daddy with lines that miraculously won his daddy a shot at a one night stand with his gorgeous mother. However, Vern saw the actor a little different than Keyshawn and his father. He hadn't cared for Carl's films made in the last thirty years. Vern loved the actor's earlier roles where he used guns and karate to take out white bigotry and anyone that created injustice for black people.

It was Carl's older movie phrases that solidified him in the streets as the movie godfather of players. Such phrases swept the streets right off of their feet, throughout America. The most memorable quote for Vern, from a flick, called Slap that Ho, which he still used, was: *"If your baby ain't got back, turn her over, Jack!"*

Today, Carl was the country's leading black actor, hands down. He's matured on screen and now plays in many romance and drama flicks. In his more recent movies, Carl served only sex education to his followers, the kind that stimulates the mind first and then the body with sometimes needless poetry and delay.

Women mostly enjoyed Carl Cleveland for his aging gentleness and stunning looks. His lines were even more so crisp, like in his last flick called Naked Booty Lovers. The movie line that got him an award nomination was: *"I know we fight all the time, but if we made love all the time instead, then we wouldn't have to fight all the time. Baby, we'd just yell for the hell of it. Now take off your clothes."*

You had to hear Carl's voice and how he said it to get the full impact. That line epitomized the max of his career for most of his longtime, romantic followers. A lot of babies were conceived on the opening night of Naked Booty Lovers, rated as a strong R.

"Whoa! Hold up! What in the hell is going on around here?"

"Keyshawn, is that Veronica getting out of Carl's car?" Vern dropped his pen and paper.

"Why in the hell is she getting out of Carl Cleveland's car?"

"Why is she adjusting her bra?"

"Why is Carl doing all that yawning and stretching? It's the middle of the day, homeboy!"

"Ooh! He is hugging your gal, Keyshawn! Know what I'm saying? That ain't no' friendly hug! He's grabbing her booty!"

Keyshawn angrily slammed his car door shut! He stomped over to his ex and the greatest black actor to ever grace the motion pictures. 'Hey! You get your damn hands off of her, brother!"

"Can I help you?" asked Carl Cleveland. "Do you want an autograph or something, boys? You're going to have to wait from across the street. Can't you see that I'm in the middle of something? I need all of this sidewalk area.... Please, use the crosswalk fellows. Thank you. Don't forget to look both ways before crossing."

"No, he didn't," whispered Vern.

"Hey!" screamed Keyshawn. "What gives, Veronica? How are you going to be getting out of a Carl Cleveland's car? Huh? More importantly, why does he have his hands all over your butt? Why are his fingers all up in your ass crack and shit? Huh? What's up with that, Veronica? And why are you all sweaty? Answer my questions!"

"Youngster, what is your boggle?" Carl asked.

Veronica turned around and said, "Oh, my goodness!"

"Oh yeah," said Keyshawn. "It's me! How could you? It only took you a week to get over me? Huh? It's like that, Veronica?"

"Yeah, Veronica!" shouted Vern. "How could you? Know what I'm saying? You're wrong, Veronica! You're wrong!"

"Bro…" Keyshawn tried to stay calm. "Carl… Will you please remove your hands from Veronica's ass? That ain't your gal!"

Veronica stepped back as Carl's hands dropped to his side.

"I guess that I didn't realize he had his hands on my butt," answered Veronica. "I was just lost in the moment. Wait, why would I need to feel like I need an excuse, Keyshawn?"

Carl smiled. He mouthed to Keyshawn, "*I tore her up.*"

"What!" Keyshawn was ready to go upside Carl's noggin. "Look here, you old geezer, you'd better watch yourself!"

One of Carl's enormous bodyguards stepped in! "You bitch-made morons need to back, the hell, up and go away."

"You had better back up!" Vern warned. "Who the' fuck are you calling morons? I dare you to touch me!"

"Is this why you haven't called me?" Keyshawn stood between Carl and Veronica. "You dropped me for him? You don't even know how many women this player has had! He'll never be with one woman. He's got every woman in his back pocket since the last supper! The man is old as dirt!"

"You've got this all wrong," said Carl. "Veronica and I are not involved. I was just pulling your leg, young man. You need to calm the hell down. I'm here to do an interview."

"He's a player!" declared Vern. "Know what I'm saying? Don't listen to that punk-ass fool, Keyshawn! Kick that sucker's ass!"

Carl pointed at Vern and said, "You're an irritating little gnat. You need to stay out of this and stop instigating."

"Irritating gangbanger?" Vern popped his knuckles and chuckled. "Um-um-um... See fool, that's okay. I can be that way, irritating and a gangster. Know what I'm saying? Those aren't necessarily problem traits in my streets. But go on and step around your bodyguard, so that I can show you five better things about me."

"Oh, whatever, you fake Malcolm X."

"What?" Vern jumped at Carl but was shoved onto the ground with ease by one of Carl's bodyguard. "Hey, man! Fuck you!"

Carl amusingly chuckled.

Exhausted from his fall, Vern said, "Carl, you need to stay out of my homeboy's business! Know what I'm saying? You've been out of the hood for too long, making too many sensitive films as of late to understand what happens when a brother tries to take another brother's bitch! Know what I'm saying? That becomes an action flick! You're out of touch with the street!"

"Blah-blah-blah," said a bodyguard. "Shut the hell up."

Veronica looked up to see her boss in the window of an office, surrounded by other nosy co-workers. They took pictures and laughed. This confrontation was good for the press! Her boss was pleased and signaled for more with her hand.

"Everybody stops!" shouted Veronica. "We're in front of my job, and I'm sure that somebody is waiting to call the cops. Now Keyshawn, this man has nothing to do with you and me. Okay? He's traveled out here from New York for an interview, so everyone needs to calm down and get out of here."

"We ain't trying to hear that!" screamed Vern. "How come you haven't called? Know what I'm saying? What's up with the tight pants on and the perfume? Where have you been all night?"

"I traveled to New York to do an interview!"

"So, how did he end up here on the west coast?"

Carl answered, "I have decided to move my latest filming here because New York is too crowded with major events at this time. Los Angeles is perfect, right now, to film the rest of my movie."

"Veronica has a car," said Vern. "Why is she carpooling with you to her job, getting out fixing her clothes? What are you wearing, Veronica? I've never seen you in grey leggings like that!"

"Is she your woman or his?" asked Carl. "You're in their business as much as I! Talk about the pot calling the kettle black! Or maybe you're just high off of some cocaine? I saw the police show last week, crack artists!"

Vern bit his lip. He snarled at Carl's bodyguards.

"How come *you haven't* called me?" Keyshawn tilted his head to the right and puckered his lips. His eyes were beady, as his eyebrows raised to his hairline. "Veronica, why haven't you called? I didn't even get a text! You had to have calmed down to talk reasonably by now. You just let me go like I was nothing!"

"I dumped your ass, Keyshawn. I don't have to talk to you ever again if I don't want to!"

"Have you slept with this… womanizer, Veronica?"

She exhaled. "It's none of your business if I've been with Carl. And he's not a womanizer! Look, Keyshawn, I feel like a broken record. I dumped you! Okay? We are no longer a couple!

Can't you understand that? I do not have to answer any of your questions."

"Dumped?" Keyshawn was a bit embarrassed. He noticed people laughing at him from all over the street. He overheard others cheer her on for moving on to Carl, obviously a better choice by reputation and looks. "What are you talking about dumped? Who me? When did you dump anyone? I wasn't dumped!"

"She didn't dump anybody!" shouted Vern over spectator boos. "She's lying! She belongs to my boy, Keyshawn. That's that! Know what I'm saying? She's saying stuff like that because she's on some heavy medication! It causes hypertensive drama in the brain! Look it up! She's drugged!"

Veronica was perplexed. "Huh? I'm not on any medication! What're you talking about, blockhead?"

"Who are you calling a blockhead?" Vern looked confused. "I know that you're not talking about me! Your mom is a blockhead!"

"I think I'll just come back later to do the interview," said Carl. He didn't want to blemish his reputation in a petty argument or an unnecessary fight. He carefully hugged Veronica again and grimaced. "All of this drama is giving me a migraine. Boy-oh-boy am' I a little stiff after that sexy yoga class we shared this morning. I think I'll go look for a masseuse and enjoy the freedoms I can afford in your town."

"Just come back later, Carl."

"No problem," replied Carl. He ignored Keyshawn and Vern. Carl climbed into his limousine. "Oh, and by the way, Veronica, you may want to fix your lipstick. It is a little smeared."

"Carl!" Veronica rubbed her lips to even her lipstick. She backed away from the limousine to avoid auto exhaust and pebbles.

Keyshawn watched the limousine roll away. "Smeared?"

"That was a hell of wrong!" declared Vern. He watched Carl's limousine drive away too, and he flipped it off. "Yeah, you'd better get out of here with that whack, old limousine. Know what I'm saying, bro? Just to think, I looked up to that chump as a kid!"

56

"Fix the lipstick?" Keyshawn was instead perplexed with Veronica's morning. "You did sexy yoga? You never did any yoga when we were together! He got to see you in some leggings doing splits and bending over, posing in downward dog and all that?"

"Yoga class has nothing to do with why I…"

Brash!

Vern heaved a rock into the back window of Carl Cleveland's limousine, which was at the nearby intersection at a red light! Glass flew everywhere, and the back of Carl's head exploded in a ball of crystals and red midst!

"What the fuck, son of a bitch!" Carl hollered. He looked at the blood on his hands that he gathered from the sore spot on his head.

"Damn." The bodyguard looked for a first aid kit in the car.

"I cannot believe this!" Carl suddenly had a frenzy of anger and slammed his fists against the door. "Look at my head! Look at my hair! Back this car up right now! Back it up! I'm going to kill that bastard!"

The limousine tires smoked and screeched, as Carl and his crew rolled backward towards the She's Golden building. When the car stopped, Carl jumped out of the limousine! He held the back of his swollen head. Blood squirted and dripped down from his S-Curl and onto the street.

"What's up?" Vern threatened. "That's how we do. Know what I'm saying? Yeah. You aren't talking much *now*, are you? I jacked your shit up, dark Gable! And I frankly don't give a damn! What? What're you going to do? Do you want some of this? What?"

"You little gangster," Carl calmly said with a smile. "I do want some, and so do my boys."

That's when the other three doors of the limousine opened. Carl was fully staffed all along. Three bodyguards got out and pulled on their black leather gloves. Nobody had called the cops yet, and if they had, the police would've made it worst for Keyshawn and Vern.

"Now what're you going to do?" Carl stepped behind his boys.

"We're going to run!" shouted Vern. "Come on, Keyshawn! Let's get the hell out of here, man! Run!"

"This big knot on my head is going to cost me a hair endorsement!" Carl hopped into the driver's seat of his limousine, ordered his guys to jump in, and he smashed the accelerator pedal!

Skurr!

"They're going to pay for this mess!" Carl declared.

"Carl!" Veronica was upset. "Carl, come back! Somebody, please call the police before those guys kill each other!"

Ms. Cobblestone casually walked out of the building and comforted Veronica. "Well, we should have expected that a thug like your ex was going to come to this low point. You need to choose your men wisely from here on out. From the looks of what I saw, you and Carl Cleveland are coming around. I like that. Did he give you a ring yet? We all know how fast celebrities work, so share the news!"

"Did you call the cops?"

"Why should I?" Ms. Cobblestone was bewildered by the question. "After all, one of your constituents is up there interviewing a Los Angeles cop right now, and he didn't even think it was necessary to protect those two thugs. They're a disgrace to our city, and they need to be behind bars. They both need to be taught a lesson and who not better to teach, than Carl Cleveland?"

"But Carl and his bodyguards are going to kill Keyshawn!"

"Doesn't Keyshawn deserve what's coming?"

By Ashaki Boelter

Veronica settled down. Her boss probably waited for her to mention that Keyshawn was worth a second of her time. Nobody needed to get fired today, especially having an exclusive interview with none other than Carl Cleveland. Veronica forcefully said, "Yeah, Keyshawn deserves what's coming. You're right as usual."

"Finally, you've come to your senses. Now, come inside."

Meanwhile, Keyshawn and Vern sprinted down another block, as Carl roared his limousine through streetlights and Stop signs.

"I have an idea," said Vern. "I'm going to hurt Carl and his punks! Know what I'm saying?"

Gasping for oxygen, Keyshawn asked, "How?"

"Just keep on running. We're almost there! We're almost…"

"We're almost where, Vern? The limousine is gaining on us! We should get off the street and cut through one of these alleys!"

"Just keep going. We're almost there!"

"I can't keep up! He's gaining on us!"

"We're almost there, Keyshawn!"

Vern suddenly came to a complete halt in front of a liquor store on the corner. "Okay, in here!"

A drunkard from across the street hailed. "Can I get a dollar?"

Keyshawn followed Vern into the liquor store. "What are you doing with that barrel?"

The liquor store owner stated, "Those are our special discounts. Do you buy it? That is a good deal. Plus, tax!"

"I'll buy the entire barrel!" Vern used his debit card to buy all of the alcohol in the barrel and for the barrel! He watched the limousine pass the store.

Carl was for sure that the thugs came around there, so he planned to make another loop around the street.

"Dude, what gives?" asked Keyshawn. "I'm not really in the partying mood. How are we going to get all of that back to the house anyway? The test drive car is parked way back at Veronica's job. What was the point of you buying all that?"

59

"The way things are going for you, you could use a drink."

"That's a lot of drinks for just me."

"Keyshawn, use your head for once. Let me handle the situation at hand. Know what I'm saying? You just look to see if you see the limousine coming back! I can hear it. It has got to be near!"

Keyshawn poked his head outside of the store entrance. "It's coming fast! We need to maybe think about finding a backdoor in case they find out we came in here. Man, they're coming fast!"

"I don't want trouble," said the store owner. "What are you two doing? Huh? I think you should leave, or I will call the cops!"

"Give us a second, dude! Damn!" Vern tilted the barrel towards the store doorway! "Look out, bro. Watch this shit."

"Vern, that's not a very good idea! What if the car gets a popped tire, swerves, and hits like the old drunkard across the street?"

"You're right. It won't work. What was I thinking? I need to get a refund. I don't even like this brand of alcohol!"

"No refund!" hollered the store clerk.

Vern wasn't paying any attention to the store clerk. "Okay, they're passing again! Get back, so they don't see us!"

"Don't do it, Vern!"

Vern poured the alcohol bottles from the barrel out into the street! *Jangle-jangle-jangle!*

Vroom! Pop! Pop! Skurr! Pop! Skurr!

"Ah!" screamed Carl, who lost control of the limousine after running over the bottles! All of the tires popped on the limo, and he and his boys spun around on sparking wheel axels and brake pads! *Whirr!*

"You stupid idiots!" hollered the shocked liquor store owner. "Look at what you dumb-dumbs done did! You're very stupid!"

Carl's limousine skidded and spun towards the building across the street, where the drunkard happily skipped into the road to collect a few bottles! "Wee! It's a flood of alcohol! It's a miracle!"

"Look out for that drunk!" shouted a bodyguard in the passenger seat of Carl's limousine. "Look out, Carl! Look out!"

"Get out of the way, you drunk bastard!" Carl placed all of his weight on the steering wheel to avoid hitting the oncoming drunkard.

After the smoke cleared, a hubcap from Carl's car rolled around the corner. The drunkard was flat on his face.

"What in the hell have you done?" screamed Keyshawn. "Vern, are you crazy? I think you killed that old drunk, dude!"

"Man, he ain't dead! I can see his finger moving, Keyshawn."

"Ah!" The injured drunkard slid away from the wreckage with a bottle of beer, while he counted dragons and mythical unicorns in the skies. He grabbed a few more bottles and placed them under his shirt and down his pants.

"You hit an old man, Carl!" The bodyguards shook out their cobwebs inside the movie star's car. "And you nearly killed us! Do you not know how to drive, brother?"

"Oh, you guys quit being sissies! The old drunkard slipped on a bottle, and I missed him. I saw it with my own eyes. I didn't hit him! If I did, he'd be dead. And I do know how to drive! Didn't you see the bottles tossed into the street by those two imbeciles?"

While the bodyguards were relieved with Carl for not hitting the drunkard and for being alive after the accident, Keyshawn was highly upset with Vern.

"Vern, how could you! Somebody could've died!"

"Man, I just saved our lives! Now, look at Carl and his fools. I say we go over there and wear them out with a few licks while they're down. I just evened the score!"

"Vern, come back!"

"Yeah, boy, you ain't doing so well now!" Vern approached the car wreckage. "I jacked you up, sucker! I guess that'll show you who not to mess with the west! Westside, you mark-ass bitch!"

Keyshawn wasn't going to let Vern fight the war alone. However, the smartest thing they could have done was run.

"You two idiots are dead!" screamed Carl. He pointed a loaded pistol at Keyshawn and Vern! "What's up now, boys?"

Keyshawn threw his hands up. "I'm sorry! I don't want to die! I just want my Veronica back! Can we please squash all of this? You go back to the movies, and I get back to my honest job. We all live happily ever after? We're both sorry for the trouble."

"Keyshawn, are you going to punk out to that high-class, sell out?" Vern was not impressed with Carl anymore. "He used to be real, back in the day. I'm what you used to stand for, Carl! You made me the player that I am today. I was your biggest fan!"

"I despise what I was," said Carl. "I killed that macho thug persona over thirty years ago! I have portrayed an intelligent black man in movies for many recent years, a gentleman, and a romancer! The majority of my base loves this guy now. You and your fellow are living in the past. We, as black folks, evolved away from those thug-killing, pimped up characters in films. Times have changed!"

"You're one of the reasons, today, as to why we don't stand together and fight against the same setbacks we had back then!" Vern was disappointed in his television hero. "It was right, to fight against the crooked system then, as it is today, you jive turkey! But then, you got fame and money. You started filming movies in Europe and sleeping with no sisters. You left your people in the struggle, which has never ended."

"I am just an actor. I am not an activist."

"Your ghetto pass has been denied. The other side can keep you, Carl Cleveland!"

"Look around you!" Carl waved his gun. "Wake up, boys! It isn't the same world anymore. We have it better today. We're now living in Martin Luther King Jr.'s dream, and that's why I make out with all kinds of hoes from other races in my movies!"

Keyshawn and Vern smacked their lips. It wasn't so long ago that they were arrested and mistreated by crooked white police.

Carl proudly made his point. "The both of you need to stop acting oppressed and pull up your pants. Start talking like you have sense and grow away from rap music into classical. Just by looking at you, Keyshawn, I can see that Veronica is out of your league. Between both of us, anyone can see why she wants to roll with me. I have a massive water bed that I plan to roll her up on and pound her on. Tonight, Veronica belongs to me!"

"Who made you so stupid?" Vern was irritated.

"My fans did," answered Carl. "And this gun pointed at you."

Vern turned to Keyshawn. "Look, that bitch dumped you. It's over. That is Carl Cleveland. We fought a good fight, but no woman on this planet is worth fighting this hard for. She'll never drop him for you. Let's just get out of here and start fresh elsewhere."

"Finally, I'm getting through to you," said Carl. "Keyshawn, you'd better listen to your hardheaded pal and step."

"Forget that, boss!" One of Carl's bodyguards spoke, "Those two nitwits tried to kill us by making us crash. They could've ended your career! Are we seriously going to just walk away from this after that damn lecture? You need to shoot one of those fools!"

Suddenly, the liquor store owner walked out of his store and onto the sidewalk with a semi-automatic gun! "Nobody is shooting anyone! Understand? Do you want to shoot someone? Take your ass down the block to'... arcade!"

"Sir!" shouted Carl. He heard the strong accent of the store owner and wanted to be clear about who he was. "Excuse me, but do you know who I am? I am a very famous actor that everybody knows. You do not want to shoot me. I'm Carl Cleveland. You've probably heard of me. I'm in huge, blockbuster movies? Do you understand? Movie... I am an actor... in movies... Understand?"

The store owner looked at Carl with disgust. He waved away Vern and Keyshawn, so they fled the scene.

Carl cautiously smiled back.

"Carl Cleveland," said the store owner, "you... you take' piece of junk car with no tire'... drive away now or... I pop your celebrity black ass! Do you understand? You get the hell off of my street! See, we don't all talk like that, and we can understand English, mother fucker! Why don't you go back to the studios and make another movie that nobody around here wants to see, you sell out!"

"How dare you talk to me like that? I'm Carl Cleveland!"

"Nobody in my family gives a damn about a Carl Cleveland," said the store owner. "You've never had a Chinese woman in your films. All I ever see you in movies with are white women! What, you don't like China nookie? Put a damn Chinese woman in your movies, asshole! Now, you and your goons take that torn up car and get off of my block before I put a cap in your old ass!"

Pop! Pop! The store owner shot bullets into the sky!

"You don't have to ask us again." Carl nodded and ordered his boys to strap in. He drove the car away on sparking wheel axels.

A bodyguard asked, "Carl, why don't you just make life simpler and drop the broad? I knew that she was a bitch from the start. And you know that you got other women to mess with."

"I like Veronica. I even think that I'm in love with her. Maybe I'm getting too old for this player shit, but she's an exceptional lady."

"She isn't worth it, boss. I'll remind you that no woman is when it comes to you. All of them only want your money."

"I don't think Veronica is about that. She was with that broke thug. I'm pretty sure that he isn't financially stable just by the way he carries himself."

By Ashaki Boelter

"I'm trying to reason with you. Are you even listening?"

"I'm not going to let those ghetto thugs outclass me and win. I'm Carl Cleveland! And today, I declare my love for Veronica."

"I know that this entire mess is going to blow up in your face, Carl, but I guess that sometimes, love just won't let go."

Chapter 6

Well, My Name is Keyshawn

"**M**an, the hos are out tonight!" Vern smacked on stale gum and adjusted his gold necklace. "You're not leaving here without a piece of ass, Keyshawn! You deserve a good time after the mess that Veronica put you through. Know what I'm saying?"

Keyshawn bobbed to the funky beats that seeped through the cracks in the walls. "Yeah, whatever dude. Look at all the ladies!"

"Midnight and this is the spot! Man, these gals are *phat* tonight! It's like a candy store up in here. I think it is Earl Mack's last night in town, so the ladies are swarming in to see him!"

"Hey, look… Isn't that Sensational Sally Sheridan from the home local improvement television show? It sure does look like her!"

"I think it is!" Vern was excited. "And… Oh, man! Look at

who is sitting alone, Keyshawn! Oh my goodness, tell me that it isn't so! Keyshawn, that's Grand Camorra, one of the hottest sisters on the local news today! Every day, I try to catch her weather report. You cannot get anymore skankier during family television hours than her!"

"Where are you looking? I don't see her."

"She's right there, man! She's the one with the big juicy tits in the middle of that crowd of bodyguards. She's about to walk into the club right now!"

"Oh yeah, I see her. I cannot believe she's here!" Keyshawn waved his hand in front of Vern. "You'd better stay away from her. Rochelle is your girl."

"Rochelle isn't here. She's in bed asleep because she has to work in the morning. Besides, I don't see any rings on my fingers. All I know is that I'd hit Grand Camorra with some wood if she asked me to. Know what I'm saying? Man, she is off the chain! Maybe you should talk to her? I guess that I should be looking out for my dude."

Minutes later, Keyshawn and Vern strutted to the bar to order drinks. It was a night of redemption, per se, for Keyshawn.

"What would you like?" asked the bartender.

"I'll have Sex on the Beach," ordered Vern.

Keyshawn was like, "I'll have a Long Island."

"Keep the tab open," added Vern, as he handed the bartender his debit card. "I'm taking care of my homeboy tonight! Whatever he needs, I'll pay for it. He got dumped for another man. Know what I'm saying? He was with that famous journalist, Veronica Evans."

"Oh yeah, I read about that. You're Keyshawn?"

"Yes, in the flesh, but let's keep that on the down-low."

"When Earl Mack makes a plan to show up, all the celebrities fill up the spot," stated the bartender. "I take it that Veronica Evans isn't here. She's quite the woman."

"Man, just get me the drink!"

"I'll make sure the drink is strong," said the bartender. "If I had lost that kind of woman, I would want to drink my brains out."

Keyshawn and Vern stood there, leaned against the bar, and browsed for future sperm depositories. Half-naked women jiggled in cages all over the club with sparkled behinds, ground up and down against the bars. The deejay spun only the newest remixes in hip-hop, and everyone was into it. The place was so off the hook. There were poker tables with hundred dollar bills that regularly fell to the floor.

Pimps and players talked smack, break-dancers popped and locked, police laughed with bouncers, virgins gave hope, married couples built memories, streetwalkers freaked, and single people mingled. There were a couple of fistfights, while some small-time celebrities signed autographs. Earl Mack and his crew gambled all night long, but it was Grand Camorra that stole the show. She was scantily dressed and invited everyone over with her eyes.

"Why don't you go over there like a gentleman and get Grand Camorra's autograph," said Vern. "I bet you can get more out of her than that. She looks a hell of hungry tonight!"

"I can't."

"What do you mean that *you can't*? Here, I just found a pen. Now take this napkin and go over to her. I know you, man. You got this! Know what I'm saying?"

"Here is your drink," said the bartender. He handed Keyshawn his Long Island. "Good luck tonight."

"She's too famous, Vern!"

"What?"

"She's way out of my league!"

"And Veronica wasn't too famous or out of your league?"

"Veronica was behind the scene. I can't do it. Forget it."

"Grow some nuts, Keyshawn!" Vern smacked his lips. "Your woman took off with Carl Cleveland. She's gone! And you know he's banging Veronica all over his hotel! You have got to let that ho go and get yours. Know what I'm saying? You got to start over!"

"Yeah, you're probably right," said Keyshawn.

"I am right! Your gal left you to fuck a star, so get your revenge by getting some from Grand Camorra! Maybe Veronica will hear about that in her celebrity circle, and she can experience your pain. Veronica ain't got' nothing' next to Grand Camorra!"

"Okay, here I go!" Keyshawn nervously walked up to Grand Camorra and her bodyguards with his drink. He began to think about Carl's advice. Maybe he should approach her with being less of the thug he is. "Hello, Grand Camorra. My name is Keyshawn. It is a pleasure to meet you."

She greeted but was unamused. "Hi, Keyshawn! Why are you talking like that? You sounded much different from the Police Tales I watched recently. That was you, right? You sounded like the cutest thug, you and your friend. I knew that show was fake! You're nothing like that guy in that episode. Maybe you can pick up a chick using your acting skills? Your soft act is not my kind of hype."

"Not true," said Keyshawn. "I don't usually come up on women like I just did. I was trying to come at you a little different to show you that I have some sense."

"Well, I don't know who told you that thugs don't have sense."

"Well, I, uh, am who you think. Yeah, I'm cool."

"Well, you're, uh, certainly not my type," she replied. "I'm all about being with real thugs, and I figured I would find one here at Earl Mack's going away party. You're too brainy. So, let's just get you my autograph so you can take it home to your mother."

"Whatever."

As she signed her name Keyshawn's napkin, her enormous breasts jiggled like oceans in a plastic bag at every stroke.

Keyshawn fell captive to her jiggling hypnotism and lost grasp of his drink! He tried to catch it, but instead, he looked as if he was Kung Fu shadow boxing her fat fake boobs.

Boing-boing-boing! The glass played pinball before sliding down between those melons of hers!

"Ah! You son of a… How? Look at what you just did!" Grand Camorra cried out. "Oh my god, it's cold! You pitiful, clumsy, bug-eyed idiot! You destroyed my favorite dress! Get the hell away from me! I ought to punch your damn lights out!"

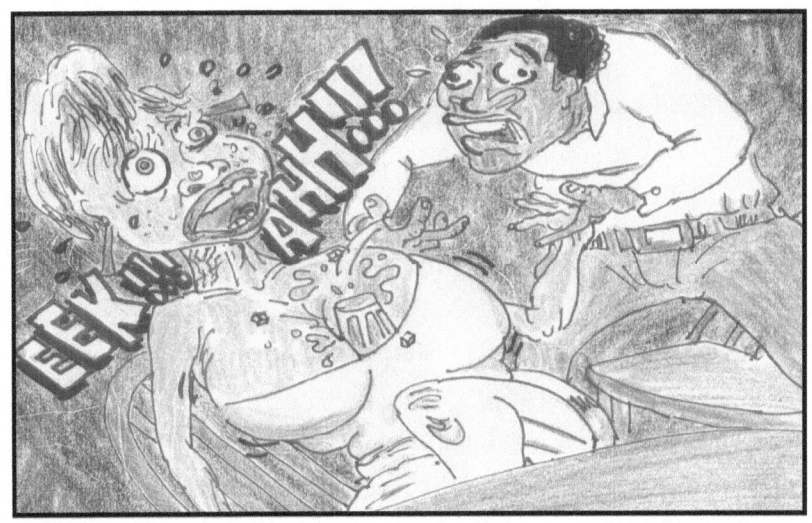

"I'm so sorry!" Keyshawn's eyes grew large as if he had a stroke! He *stood up* straight and stared down her drenched, twin cities. He was so shocked at the most fabulous breasts he'd ever seen that he didn't bother to try and wipe them dry. "Great Scott, those are huge!"

"What in the hell are you doing, you pervert?" shouted one of her bodyguards, who used his jacket to cover up the celebrity's nippily wet top. "You get the hell away from her!"

Grand Camorra added, "I heard Veronica Evans dumped you; I can see why! You're an idiot, you asshole!"

Another one of her bodyguards stepped to Keyshawn's face.

"I'm sorry!" Keyshawn repeated. "It was an accident!"

Keyshawn embarrassingly strutted back to Vern.

"Way to go!" Vern celebrated and laughed. "You got her knockers drenched, and that had every cell phone camera in the club going off! Do you want to see the shot I got? You're a legend around here now! Know what I'm saying? That was genius!"

"You're crazy, Vern! I'm glad your girlfriend doesn't hear half the stuff you tell me. So, why aren't you gambling yet?"

"Of course, I'm gambling! I made a bet with the bartender here that you'd leave with Grand Camorra. Know what I'm saying?"

"You're just giving money away now. Are you for real?"

The bartender smiled. "Young man, you're clumsy, and you've got no backbone. That's why your woman left you. I just made one hundred bucks from your friend here. Who is your next target? I have rent to pay."

"Hey, you told this stranger about my business!" Keyshawn wasn't going to get dissed anymore by Vern or the bartender. "Forget the both of you. I'm not a game or some kind of entertainment for you or the rest of the world!"

"Your friend is nuts," stated the bartender.

Vern tried to calm his dude. "You're cracking, homeboy. You ain't supposed to let no chick get you to this level! Keep it together."

"Keep it together? What! Over the last week, Vern, you have fucking embarrassed me and made me feel like a fucking loser!"

"I don't make you feel like a loser. Maybe you shouldn't drink anymore. I think the bartender made your drink too strong."

The bartender walked away, "Don't look at me. Your friend has lost his damn mind."

"Fuck you, bartender! I haven't lost my mind!"

"You should look in the mirror before you start pointing at others," argued Vern. He waved away the bartender, who was about to kick Keyshawn out for cussing at him. "Keyshawn, you're the one who takes all the ill-advised risk. And when you do win, you don't even see the victory and dwell in a loss. With Veronica, maybe sometimes, love won't let go, but you have to know when to quit."

"Quit? I don't quit."

"I told you the day you met that she just needed comfort until she got over her ex. You didn't listen, and you went all in for her within weeks. She didn't truly love you; she just had you to maintain her sexual needs."

"None of that is true! She did love me!"

"No, she didn't!" Vern shouted. "If she did, you wouldn't be sleeping on my damn couch!"

"You know what, Vern? I'm out of here!"

"Hey man, hold on!" Vern grabbed Keyshawn's arm. "I'm

your closest homie. What's up, man?"

"You think everything is a game! Let go of my arm!"

"You deserve that gal over there," added Vern. "I can help you fix that. She'll for sure get your mind off of Veronica!"

"No! I need to get away from you!"

"Keyshawn, we've been tight since elementary. Know what I'm saying? I know you better than you know yourself! You're bugging right now. Calm the hell down!"

"What? You don't know me."

"Good Lord! Do I need to order you a cup of coffee from next door? Know what I'm saying? It's the drink talking."

"I'm not drunk, Vern. I spilled most of my drink on Grand Camorra's boobs. Remember?"

"Oh, yeah, that's right."

"I am not interested in a one-night affair, Vern. It was Veronica that showed me how good a real relationship feels. Where do those women exist in a club like this? You go on and play; I'll be out in my car napping until you're ready to leave. I need some air."

"You need a psychiatrist!" Vern was suddenly aware that plenty of people watched him and Keyshawn, as the music broke into another song. He had a club reputation and would have the last word with Keyshawn.

"I need to see a shrink?"

"What happened to you, Keyshawn? Veronica messed your head up the moment she opened her legs, man! But she screwed you to the maximum, showing up to her job with Carl Cleveland."

Grand Camorra and other gossipers overheard that. She asked, "Carl Cleveland and Veronica Evans are together?"

"Vern, why are you spitting all my business out in the open? You're always trying to get up on me."

"Nobody cares about our business here! Know what I'm saying? Nobody knows us."

"Then I guess it is okay for me to say that I think it was a bad idea for you to purposely roll those bottles onto the street to cause a car accident that could've killed Carl Cleveland. That car accident could have killed an innocent bystander too!"

The bartender whispered, "He tried to kill Carl Cleveland, the coolest action actor of 1970's black cinema?"

"You need to be quiet!" Vern looked around the club. None of the police heard Keyshawn. "What the hell are you trying to do here, get me arrested? Know what I'm saying? Keep that shit on the low!"

"You want to tell my business; I will tell yours."

"Fuck you, Keyshawn!" Vern held his middle finger to his friend's face. "You are a damn loser."

Keyshawn slapped Vern's hand.

"Kick his ass, Vern!" The bartender was all for it.

"What's up then, son?" Vern invited Keyshawn.

"You ruined my life, you ass!" Keyshawn challenged.

Right then, a person nearby intentionally bumped Vern into Keyshawn! The two friends violently grappled and choked each other over small tables and chairs. Earl Mack grabbed his money and left the club, as they rolled onto the dance floor. They punched and cursed until the bouncers grabbed them by their necks.

"And stay out!" The bouncers threw Keyshawn and Vern out the front door of the club.

Vern brushed off the street dust and strutted towards Keyshawn's car. "Screw you, Key! You can catch a ride-share or cab! Know what I'm saying? Just sleep it off for now, and we'll talk about this shit in the morning!"

"Hey! That's my car!" Keyshawn realized that Vern took his keys during the scramble. "You'd better not touch my car, fool!"

Skurr!

"I'll leave the front door unlocked!" Vern drove off in Keyshawn's car and nearly gave himself whiplash.

Keyshawn flipped Vern the bird. Shit happened. He cooled enough to know friends don't always agree, and sometimes, thugs took it there. Yet, when he reached into his pocket, his wallet and cell phone were stolen by Vern too.

So, he sat against the wall and watched the moon surf over the stars for hours until the club closed. It was tranquil and so dark in the wee morning. There was not one car that drove by him.

"Are you okay?"

Keyshawn kept his head down. "Doesn't that seem obvious?"

"Did you have a bad day or what?"

"Leave me alone, bitch. I don't need comfort in a hooker."

"I'm a hooker? Look, can I give you a lift somewhere?"

"No. Can you just leave me alone?"

"Let me help you up from the ground? You surely don't want to sit there all night on that hard concrete. You'll freeze."

"Hey, Olivia!" shouted a voice from inside the club. "We'd best be going now. Where are you? You have an important television interview in the afternoon. Olivia?"

"I'm just out front getting some fresh air, Frank. The alley in the back was a bit smelly with all that garbage. Look, just swing the car out front. I'll be waiting for you up here!"

"I just want to be left alone," said Keyshawn. "Thank you."

"I know that it was an accident with your drink spilling all over my chest. And about your friend, I understand stuff happens. I'm also sorry that I called you an idiot and that you deserved to be dumped."

Keyshawn looked up to validate who the anti-Christ might be. He was surprised! He cleared up his ugly attitude fast. "You're Grand Camorra! I'm sorry. I didn't know it was you. I heard the guy inside call you Olivia. What's up with that?"

"Olivia is my real name," she answered. "I've told Frank to stop calling me that in public. I guess since the club is closed, he thought it was okay. Look, it's cold out here, and I do know the forecast for the morning is light showers. After all, I am an operational meteorologist too. I assume that you live around here, can I give you a lift home or something?"

"Okay. Well, yes!"

Olivia's limousine suddenly pulled up in front of them.

"Go on," said Keyshawn. "Ladies go first."

Olivia got in the car, and it suddenly drove away with the door wide open! Frank requested her to close the door as he high-fived the driver and laughed about nearly taking Keyshawn's leg off.

"We can't just leave him there," said Olivia to the limousine driver. "I offered to give him a ride home."

"Unless you're paying us over time, we're taking you straight back to the hotel. That guy was a whack job. We don't need to be picking up his kind. Everybody saw him on Police Tales, and I watched the pervert intentionally spill his drink all over you."

The driver agreed with Frank. "Yeah, he was sick."

"Your shift is over, driver." Olivia was annoyed. "Pull over the car and get out."

"What are you doing?" asked Frank. "You can't just get rid of your driver. Just because you're a popular weather forecaster that is getting support roles in various movies, doesn't make you all that powerful. You cannot be treating him like that!"

"You're right, Frank. You get out of the car also."

"What?" Frank was shocked. "I'm your bodyguard!"

"Well, you can bodyguard yourself out of the car. Consider that you both have the rest of the morning off for being jerks. That guy back there was going through it; you try having a heart!"

The limousine driver pulled over to the side of the road and exited. "At least we're not fired."

"This is insane!" shouted Frank, who stood next to the driver. "You can't just leave us in the middle of the ghetto, Olivia!"

"Why can't I?"

"It's dangerous! We could get jumped."

"With muscle and guns, you'll both be alright. Call a cab. I'll see you both in the afternoon."

"Olivia, you are a desperate whore! Just make sure to wear

76

protection!" Frank pulled his cell out as he watched her drive away.

Skurr!

Within five minutes, Olivia's limousine rolled back up to the club. "Are you sure I can't give you a lift, Keyshawn? The club lights are out, and it is cold out here. Come on!"

"You're not going to drive off the minute I touch the door handle?" Keyshawn got in the passenger seat of the limousine. "What happened to your guys?"

"They took another way back to the hotel," she replied. "I did not appreciate what they did, driving away like that. I'm sorry. Say, I didn't drink much tonight, and I know you didn't. How about you and I stop by the liquor store? I saw it on the corner up there; we can load up a few drinks. As I say, when it rains, it is time to pour."

Keyshawn saw that she tried to cheer him up. He also noticed that he was now in front of the same liquor store that he and Vern visited earlier.

"What's wrong? You look as if you saw a ghost, Keyshawn."

"Olivia, if I may call you that, you're going to have to go get the drinks in that store without me."

"Sure, that's fine, but why not come in the store with me?"

"Let's just say that my pal from the club put an end to that."

"I won't even ask. Your friend was a dick at the club." Olivia took a deep breath. "Is there a favorite drink I can get you?"

"I'll have what you're having."

After Olivia returned from the liquor store with a bag full of bubbly and a couple of cases of dark beer, they cruised through the Ventura Hills and then parked upon a hidden peak that looked down into the Pacific Ocean that harbored sharks and killer octopus. As the moonlight shined upon the two and the endless sea waves entertained, Keyshawn and Olivia felt safe around one another. Together, they shared, laughed, drank, talked, touched, and enjoyed one another's company.

"So, what do you do for a living?" Olivia asked.

"I work down at the factory outside of town. I scan and stow products, but mostly deliver."

"That's admiral work," replied Oliva. "Boy, I sure do miss genuinely real people. I've been in a celebrity and Hollywood industry for so long. I love it too, but… Sometimes, I want to be able to just go to a mall without being recognized. It's not always a blessing to be a celebrity of any sort. That's why I have a bodyguard watching my every step, everywhere I go."

Keyshawn chuckled. "Well, it probably doesn't help that you're so hot. I can't blame your bodyguard for *watching* you so much? Can you hire me too?"

"Oh my goodness," laughed Olivia, "you're so funny and a pervert I might add!"

"How did you know my mom's maiden name?"

"What?" Olivia giggled more. "You're stupid or drunk!"

"Yes, they call me Keyshawn Stupid Drunk Pervert. That's my name. Don't wear it out. So, Olivia, I see you on the news from time to time, but how do you make out these days?"

"Excuse me? No, you didn't!"

"I'm talking about your career!" Keyshawn smacked his forehead. "I meant, how is your career coming? I don't recall seeing you on any television shows, except the news, for at least the last five or six years."

"That is a very long story, but I do have some thankfully uncredited roles," answered Olivia. She hurriedly changed the story. "So, I can see that you're not at all like the thug I saw on that police show. You're not as mean as the show made you out to be."

"We got pulled over that night," explained Keyshawn, "and next thing we knew, a van full of actors in police uniforms and our clothing got out and made a show of it."

"Wait. So Police Tales isn't real?"

"Nope," answered Keyshawn. "Those shows have directors, makeup artists, and a big production crew at the scene. The only thing those shows do is make low class, and minority people look like wild animals. Those shows are a protagonist of racial diseases in our

By Ashaki Boelter

world; they make fun of people's race, creed, sex, or misfortunes for entertainment. They should get rid of all of those kinds of shows!"

"So, what's up with Veronica Evans dumping you? You seem like a good dude with some sense. A lot of celebrities would love to have a normal good guy at home. What's wrong with her?"

Keyshawn downed another beer.

"Well, she was a fool to leave you," said Olivia. "You certainly bring hope back into the whole dating scene for me."

"I'm no angel. I assure you of that. I'm just a normal dude."

"I haven't dated for some time because the guys I have come across in the industry are evil," Olivia slurred. "So, you're an angel to me. I guess we're on the same page with all our troubles. Misery loves company, doesn't it? Well, it is coming to that time for me to retire for the night because I have a plane to catch later this afternoon. Maybe we should pick up this conversation when I return in a couple of days if you don't mind?"

"Olivia, are you totally wasted and just talking, or would you be interested in talking to a brother again like that?"

"Wasted? No. At least I don't think so."

"So, I am being filmed or recorded to destroy my image in tabloids? Everybody seems to be up in my business since getting dumped by Veronica Evans."

Olivia shook her head, no. "Look around. It's just you and I."

"Yeah, it is just you and I..."

Olivia leaned over him to his enjoyment of her rack all up in his face, and she gnawed on his left ear! She poked her tongue throughout every waxed fiber of his hairy earhole, as he suddenly felt the urge to have an orgasm. Her warm breath worked its way down his neck, under his shirt, and cooked his hardened nipples. Then she suddenly passed out, and her head slid down his chest and onto his lap!

"Olivia?" Keyshawn was surprised that she didn't poke her eye out upon a crashing impact with his groin, which almost caused a silent splash. "Um... Oh, snap! Oh my goodness, her hair smells so good. Olivia?"

79

Olivia quickly sat up. "I'm sorry! I must have nodded off. Keyshawn, I think I'm drunk. We may have to sleep this off right here unless you can drive. I don't even know where the hell we are."

Keyshawn looked out his window. "Shit. Where are we?"

They both laughed at mosquitos that landed on the window and played music trivia using the car horn.

"I'm having the time of my life, Keyshawn."

"Me too," replied Keyshawn. "Maybe we should stop drinking, though. Olivia, you're looking kind of pale."

"I'm a ghost," she declared and laughed. "Watch me become invisible. Boom! You cannot see me now because I disappeared."

"I can see you, Olivia. Are you sure that you're feeling okay?"

"*Humph! Oh god!* I think I got to puke!" Olivia yelped like an angered whale and violently vomited all over Keyshawn, partially undigested chunks of stomach guts as tremendous as tater tots splattered in near mayo substances! The acidic drool that swung from her expanded lips splattered all over Keyshawn's tensed face, and that caused him also to vomit until he finally passed out. Olivia threw up so much that she passed out as well from dehydration. The two snored the night away, drenched in sizzling, gooey vomit, a bonding solution of what they both lacked in companionship: Privacy.

So they thought.

Chapter 7

Landmines and Goldmines

"So, how was yoga this morning?" Ms. Cobblestone walked up to Veronica's desk for some girl talk and the scoop on her with Carl Cleveland. After all, any rumors made for a good story and higher ratings for the company. And Ms. Cobblestone was all about money.

"It was good this morning." Veronica massaged her neck.

"Did you get a sore neck from this morning or last night?"

"Excuse me, Ms. Cobblestone?"

Ms. Cobblestone leaned in. "You are dating Carl Cleveland, and you're using yoga to cover his prowess under the sheets. Veronica, I too would need more time in the morning before work if I had a Carl Cleveland. I get it. You earned the right to be late."

"We're not like that. Carl is just there to help me through this time in my life. We found that we have some things in common, so we're just friends... going to yoga classes."

"You're not giving him any coochie? Why is he even in our town when he is supposed to be filming in New York?"

Veronica sighed. "He said New York was too crowded to do filming because of the annual sports extravaganza and the king is there. He instructed that his production crew come out here to check out some spots to film instead."

"But, you're not giving up anything in the meantime?"

"We're not doing anything."

"So, he's taking you to yoga every morning, brings you to work, takes you to lunch, got you those cards on your desk, and nothing is going on between you both?"

"Nothing," answered Veronica. "He's just a friend."

"I'm not into women myself, but Veronica, I see your body every day, and you're pretty put together. There isn't any way he's not fantasizing about what he sees of you in those yoga classes. So, don't be surprised when he makes a move on you, girl!"

"I cannot believe you get away with talking to your staff about these things, as my boss."

"We're a gossip company," replied Ms. Cobblestone. She sat upon Veronica's desk, with one buttock. "I wouldn't care if it weren't Carl Cleveland, but he's public domain. I need to know all of the details, as well as his fans. It helps the revenue of his films when fans read all the hype about their favorite actors. We go hand in hand with the success or failure at the box office."

Veronica picked up her phone and dialed anybody. She noticed that other office employees were all up in her business.

"Veronica, you aren't still trying to work on keeping that thug you had, right?" Ms. Cobblestone asked. "I sense you're hesitant with Carl, for no logical reason. I told you to drop that ex thug!"

"Oh no, that chapter is closed with Keyshawn!"

"What's the holdup, Veronica? You've got the hottest actor in the world in the palm of your hands! You haven't had a real man in ages!"

"I don't know. I'm not ready for another relationship yet."

Ms. Cobblestone rejected that notion. "All you have to do is take Carl Cleveland for one pony ride, and you'll become ready!"

"I'm just not ready for *that*."

"Well, maybe this brand new issue of Celeb Daily, from this morning, will get you ready?" Ms. Cobblestone slammed down a gossip magazine onto Veronica's desk!

"What is going on there on the cover, Ms. Cobblestone?"

"That's your ex-boyfriend Keyshawn, and according to the story inside, that woman is hot weathergirl, Grand Camorra!" Ms. Cobblestone became furious. "Yeah, that's right. All you see is the back of her head between his knees. You know what went on there before they passed out: Blow city! If Keyshawn could move on, why can't you?"

Veronica realized that sometimes, love just wouldn't let go because she had an itch of jealousy.

Ms. Cobblestone continued to go off. "This issue is selling out like mad this morning according to my inside sources! Nobody is buying our magazine this morning! Also, your ex is now trending all over social media and the Internet at number one!"

Veronica studied the picture with disgust and listened with scolded feelings. It certainly was Keyshawn.

"The Paparazzi got this great photo shot from a helicopter this morning, and you can even see that there's a liquid stain all over his lap; you and I both know what that is, Veronica!" Ms. Cobblestone placed her hands on her hips.

"Keyshawn…"

"Grand Camorra, one of the nastiest whores on television fronting as a family-oriented weathercaster, has a notorious record of doing this to men from what I've heard. Rumor has it that men never get past her oral pleasures, with her big old lips. She's like a vacuum cleaner and makes men explode before third base. And there is your ex, Keyshawn, in all of his glory and your reputation."

"I'm sorry. I just cannot believe that Keyshawn would do that. He's better than that!"

Ms. Cobblestone shook her head. "Why are you so blind and still sticking up for that thug? He's nothing more than an imbecile that lucked out with getting in your panties. I'll tell you one thing, though. He's not better than Carl Cleveland or your most valuable player before him. Look at that tasteless picture. You made a sicko like him get access to celebrity status by dating you."

Veronica felt that Ms. Cobblestone was right about Keyshawn, and it was evident from the picture that she should have maybe heeded her boss's advice. "You were right from the start."

"You made a mistake dating a careless idiot, Veronica!" Ms. Cobblestone pounded her fist on Veronica's desk. "I warned you before you even decided to let him in. Now, he's all over the news! He's America's newest bad boy, and it makes you look like an ex whore! How does that make our reputation around here look?"

"I think…"

"Who is going to buy a magazine with articles written from a bunch of so-called whores, Veronica? When people think of whores, they don't think of educated journalists! They think of brainless, cheap sluts! It is one thing to be a magazine sold for men's pleasure, but we're not that company! Our journalism belongs in every home, for all ages and types! Can you imagine a dad's daughter coming across your article and that same dad takes the magazine away from his daughter because you wrote an article? After all, he devalues your opinion sorely based on how you live your life whoring with losers like Keyshawn."

"I didn't think…"

"That's right! You didn't think, Veronica!" Ms. Cobblestone had the entire office's attention. "Now that he's making the news, with such stars as yourself and now Grand Camorra, it makes sense for us to interview him. That's our job, isn't it?"

"Yes."

"We interview the freshest, newest, and up and coming!"

"Okay, right."

"So, who is to say that you're not put on an assignment to interview Keyshawn?" Ms. Cobblestone looked into Veronica's eyes. "He made the front page of the Celeb Daily, for goodness sakes! If he keeps going at this pace, sleeping with more celebrities…"

"You wouldn't."

"I would put you on assignment to interview Keyshawn without hesitation, unless… you get me the story that I *really* wanted yesterday!"

"You got it, anything you want."

"I want the dirty-dirty about Carl Cleveland!" Ms. Cobblestone rubbed her hands together; she was the badass of blackmail and manipulation. "I don't care if it is you making the story happen while hammering his brains out! You just get me my story and the dirty pictures! Veronica, there will be great compensation and a bonus for you. Just do your job! That'll be all, so get back to work."

Veronica watched her boss slide off the edge of her desk and joyfully strolled into her office. The Celeb Daily paper sat there upon her desk, but something else suddenly took her undivided attention.

No, it wasn't the condensation of Ms. Cobblestone's dirty butt crack evaporating at an increasing rate along with the shitty foul smell.

With eyes of flames, Veronica stood from her desk and approached Devon, who mingled at the water fountain.

"You little jerk," she harshly whispered at him. Veronica snatched his cup of water and threw it at Devon! "I have been waiting to do that all week, jerk! You're lucky that I've cooled off, while you took a vacation or leave. You almost made me believe that you took time away to hide from me after the stunt you pulled!"

"Why the hell did you throw my cup of water at me? Okay, yes, I did go on vacation. I went to Maui. But what's gotten under your skin besides Ms. Cobblestone? And why would I have to hide from you?"

"Devon, I ought to break your flipping nose!"

Devon acted as if he didn't know what happened in her recent interview that he set up with the king. "Dear friend, let's talk it out over dinner!"

"You tried to set me up with that jerk of a king? Why in the hell would you do that? And don't you even lie! You told me I'd get the interview of my life! Do you realize that he tried to take advantage of me, Devon? All I wanted to get was an interview, but he wanted to screw me against my will! You set up a camera crew that could've cared less. Then the king mentioned that you were behind setting me up for sex, like some kind of pimp! Just who do you think you are?"

"Keep it down! It's not a good place to talk about this."

"Fuck you, Devon! I thought I was your friend!"

"You are," Devon whispered. "I didn't know that he was going to go at you like that. I thought he was going to be intelligent about helping you get over your ex-boyfriend while doing the interview. He's got a track record about helping women get past their exes. I needed you to get over the hump with your thug ex-boyfriend."

"I'm no idiot," replied Veronica. "I know that you have a crush on me. Why couldn't you have been smart enough just to try and be that guy for me? I was vulnerable at the time, and you're someone I trusted. Man, for working the relationship columns for this

86

company, you're so damn stupid!"

"I'm not stupid," Devon whispered. "Maybe I just didn't want to be your rebound guy! Okay? Look, you introduced your ex-boyfriend, Keyshawn, to me at the last award ceremony. Do you believe that, since you dumped him, that I would want to be the guy next in line for him to figure as the one responsible for your decision to dump him? I needed you to be rebounded before I jumped all in it. Excuse me for planning a safer way to your heart!"

"What? Do you realize how stupid you sound?"

"I'm smart enough to know that he'd beat the shit out of me if he saw me with you right after you dumped him! I saw him in that police episode. Keyshawn was crazy! I'm a lover, not a fighter."

"You are such a weak bitch, Devon. I could have used your company! I trusted you. The king tried to violate me!"

"I only directed you to him to do an interview. Anything criminally outside of that, I had nothing to do with. Maybe you should've gone to the police instead of leaving with Carl Cleveland."

"Maybe I wouldn't have if you'd had some balls and asked me out in the first place."

"Whoa, hey guys!" greeted Hugo, the closest friend of Devon. He walked up behind both of them and placed them in a bear hug. "We love each other! You both may want to keep it down. Ms. Cobblestone is looking at you both through her blinds from her office. Let's just slow our roles here and return to a professional journalism atmosphere before jobs are lost."

"Devon," said Veronica with her lip turned up, "don't you ever talk to me again! Don't even look in my direction. I ought to cut your ass! I mean it. You just stay the hell, far away from me!"

Devon was utterly turned off, as Veronica walked away. He held up his middle finger and whispered, "Forget you too, Veronica."

Hugo laughed like a chipmunk. He stepped in front of Devon and cleared his throat. "Look at all that ass; you know you want to take that back. How can you forget all that? Look at it!"

"I'm done with her, Hugo."

"Let me show you how I think you should have done this from the start, Devon. I mean, I overheard that she is not dating Carl Cleveland anyways. That does not mean she didn't already get screwed. That means that I would not be the rebound guy. The hell if I'm going to let that ass slip away. If you don't want her, you can step aside and watch a pro now, Devon."

Devon watched his friend approach Veronica. Hugo said, "Hey, Veronica, I'm sorry about what just went down over there between Devon and yourself. I also heard that you and Carl Cleveland are not a couple. Look, I was wondering if maybe you and I could go out sometime."

"Hell no, we cannot go out!" Veronica lifted her fists and jerked with her shoulders at Hugo as if she was going to punch his lights out. She then stormed off to the restroom.

"What the fuck?"

"She's not worth it," said Devon. "She once told me that she was raised in the ghetto side of town. Well, that showed when she told me she wanted to cut me. Man, I'm staying away from that gangster girl! I wasn't raised in that kind of atmosphere. She probably belonged to a gang at some point, across town. You know, maybe Devon was the right kind of guy after all, and we were wrong to have fantasized the kind of guy for her based on her looks."

Hugo added, "Yeah, we talked so negatively about him around here that we encouraged her to leave him sublimely and in every other way, time and time again. What if she and Keyshawn were meant to be, but now she couldn't go back. We messed all that shit up."

"She did seem happy with him," said Devon. "We should have just stayed out of it. Now, she's just one angry woman."

Meanwhile, across town from all that ignorance was a heap of rundown apartments and homes shortly built after the factories and warehouses went up outside of the city. Right smack in the middle of the low-income town was Vern's duplex.

Despite what those in upper areas felt about the area via hungry news outlets and driving by themselves, this side of town was a place of comfort, family, a place of many faiths, and shared responsibility to the community between the people. It had its rough edges, along with any neighborhood. Even so, Vern and Keyshawn's hood was always positively active on Saturday mornings, starting at eight o'clock AM on the dot!

Black-owned businesses and entrepreneurs did their best to uplift and strengthen the communities by offering plenty of services, such as counseling, shelter, medical assistance, and food all the time. However, not everyone was receptive to his or her privacy, so the occasional knocks in the early morning were not always welcomed.

Bang-bang-bang!

"Who in the hell is knocking at the front door so hard and this early?" Keyshawn sat up on the couch that Vern let him sleep on for a minute until he could find an apartment.

Bang-bang!

Keyshawn flung open the front door. "Can I help you?"

"Good morning," greeted the tidy man in a suit at the door. Behind him, his wife and kid stood with smiling faces. In his arms, he held a few church pamphlets and a bible. "I'm Erickson Lowery, and this is my wonderful family. We're representing the Jehovah's..."

Slam!

"Get the hell out of here," said Keyshawn. He stumbled back to the couch. "It's too early for all that. I got a headache from the stuff I drank last night."

"You're going to hell, young man!" Erickson threatened from the porch. "It's the end day!"

Bang-bang! Bang-bang-bang!

Keyshawn fiercely opened the door. "Man, if you don't get the..." He stopped in mid-speech. There was somebody else at his door. So he asked, "Can I help you?"

"Hello sir, my name is Charlotte Brown, and I'm from the First Greater Pentecostal Holiness of... Wait!"

Slam!

Charlotte flew from the porch after the door slammed into her face; she cussed her hair off, literally. She picked up her wig and also walked to another residence to spread the gospel.

Keyshawn headed to the kitchen for an ice pack. His back ached because Vern's old couch was uncomfortable. It was only three hours since Olivia dropped him off, but he still smelled her vomit in his pores. He decided it was a good idea to take a shower now.

Bang! Bang-bang-bang-bang!

"I can't believe this!" declared Keyshawn. He returned to the front door. He opened it, and there stood three middle school girls. "Can I help you, kids?"

"Hi," greeted one of the girls. "We represent the Big Girls of National Alliance, and we're selling cookies to raise money for our trip to Mexico. Would you help support us by buying a box of one of our delicious cookie selections?"

"What kind of cookies do you have?"

"We have chocolate chip, mint chip, peanut butter, and coconut cookies. Would you like to buy a box of cookies?"

"How much are you selling them for?"

"There are 18 cookies to a box for $25. That's a good deal for such tasty cookies!"

"That's a lot of money for some damn cookies."

One of the girls whispered to another, "He must be broke. Doesn't anyone around here have money?"

"So, mister, do you want to buy a box to help us make the trip?"

"Hold on. I'll be right back." Keyshawn nicely closed the door and walked to the kitchen. He grabbed a bag of cookies from a cabinet and returned to the front door. He opened it. Then he reached into his package and pulled out his cookie and ate it in their faces.

The girls stared in amazement. "You are a jerk, sir."

"But you're the one selling a little box of cookies for $25," replied Keyshawn. "Get the hell out of here." Then he reached into his cookie bag and grabbed another to eat. Crumbs and chips drizzled from his lips as he loudly moaned with extreme delight and satisfaction. "These three-dollar cookies are so good. Umm - ump! You girls wouldn't happen to be selling any milk, would you? I sure could use a glass."

"How dare you act so rude to some kids?" One of the girls was utterly fluttered. "We're selling cookies for a great cause, and all you're doing is standing there and being an ass this morning!"

"Oh, I'm an ass, you little shit?"

"Yes!"

Slam!

Keyshawn grew angrier, not because of the morning soliciting, but because he realized that he forgot to ask Olivia for her phone number, and he did not get any last night.

Suddenly, the front door swung open with a key in it. Vern entered his apartment, full of energy! He declared, "Keyshawn, you are the man! Know what I'm saying? This paper is out all over the neighborhood! The Paparazzi captured you and Grand Camorra doing the nasty! You have got to tell me how it was! Look at that freak!"

"Say what? Hold up!"

"Look at this paper. There you are, and there the bitch is!"

That's when Vern's house phone suddenly rang. He walked over to it, but there was no listing on the caller ID to know who it was.

The phone ring ceased. Then it started up again.

"Hello?" Vern irritatingly answered. "No, this isn't him. However, he's standing right next to me. Why? You're tripping, bitch! How are you trying to raise hell in here? Know what I'm...? What? Fuck you too!"

"Who is that?" asked Keyshawn.

"Just take the phone. I can't even see straight, bro."

"Hello?"

The female voice barely squirted out, "How could you? I thought... Are you trying to get back at me because I dumped you?"

Keyshawn knew who it was. "Well, Veronica, I'm not going to sit around and watch you have all the fun! And what are you calling for anyways? Oh, are you trying to start some shit? Why didn't I answer my cell phone? I don't have to answer that!"

Vern apologized. "I had your phone, dude. There wasn't any way in hell I was answering her calls. Here's your cell phone back."

"Bet."

"Man, hang up on that bitch." Vern paraded around his living room like he'd had enough and wanted to place a cap in somebody. "Tell her never to call my house phone again! Tell her to lose my number because nobody hurts my homeboy like that! Know what I'm saying? Fuck that bitch!"

Keyshawn hung up the phone.

"Wait!" Veronica wanted to hear Keyshawn's voice for seconds more, as sometimes, love just wouldn't let go. "Hello? Keyshawn, are you there? Hello?"

Ms. Cobblestone walked up to Veronica's desk. "This is your overtime day; I don't pay time and a half on Saturdays to make personal calls to your ex. Veronica, you've got to let that thug go. There's no sense in sweating him. Did you see the picture of the woman with her lips around his you-know-what? He cheated on you, and there's no telling what she gave him."

"I was just calling to see how he was making out."

"Veronica! Why would you? He's making out just fine and all. You're making yourself look pretty stupid."

"Ms. Cobblestone, he's not a bad person. Sure, he has some street mentality. He's also a human being that has been there for me, time and time again. Maybe this thing is a big misunderstanding? I haven't taken the time to hear him out. I may have overreacted and wrongly threw him out."

"What? You just need to get it in your thick skull that he's repulsive and makes terrible decisions. That's the bottom line. And like I said, it was your job or him. You chose your job."

"I guess that sometimes, love just won't let go. You know?"

"He deserved to be dumped for how he treated you from the start," added Ms. Cobblestone. "I know you're a Christian and all, but you shouldn't be so forgiving. Men like him are the ones that get away with battery and rape because women are too afraid to stand up and do the right thing by leaving them."

"I guess that you're right, again."

"I'm always right, darling." Ms. Cobblestone turned away but stood near Veronica's desk. "It's time for you to be happy with a man. It's time for you to double your money with Carl Cleveland! You have the sexiest man on the planet, and you're contemplating keeping him? You need to sweat Carl Cleveland until he proposes to you! Go on now, pick up the phone and *call him.* I will honor that on company time, as he has granted us an interview already."

"Why are you so infatuated with me getting with Carl?"

"I was once married to a motorcycle thug," Ms. Cobblestone explained. "For fifteen years, I tried to do marriage his way, as he loved to ride his motorcycle with a gang six days a week. Eventually, he'd come home and beg me to have his kid, since he sensed I was on my way out and was losing control. And he certainly was because I slept with many of his friends. His behavior ruined me and my own decisions in life. I don't want to see that happen to you."

"Keyshawn was not like that; he wanted to be around me all

the time. He never neglected me like your ex, Ms. Cobblestone. I never wanted to sleep around when I was with Keyshawn. And in all fairness, that picture in the magazine was taken after I dumped him."

"All thugs are the same," stated Ms. Cobblestone. "At some point, if he hadn't already slapped you around, he was going to resort to violence upon disagreements soon. I saved you the trouble by keeping you busy around here. We don't need those kinds of men, Veronica. You don't want a landmine; you want a goldmine! And now, you've got Carl Cleveland."

"Yeah, but how long are you going to live in another person's glory when it comes to men?'

Ms. Cobblestone puckered in disagreement. "Do you think that I don't have a good man? Well, be it as it may, contrast to all of what employees think, I don't usually spill my business around here. However, since you and I are on the level, I'll fill you in that next week I'm going to Paris with a very nice man named Gus Drew. That information does not leave the conversation between you and me."

"Gus Drew? You're dating the bodybuilding gold medalist?"

"He's been rocking my world for about five weeks now."

"Wait. Ms. Cobblestone, isn't he married?"

"Not a word to anyone," told Ms. Cobblestone. "And if you hadn't noticed, I've been getting heat flashes ever since I've been sleeping with him."

Veronica reflected on the wet butt streak Ms. Cobblestone left on her desk yesterday. "Yep, I noticed."

"He just makes me wet, talking about him. Whoa!"

"Carl is alright. He doesn't share enough for me to know much about him, except that he is interested."

"Why should he have to? He's in all encyclopedias and Internet databases. There are plenty of interviews about his personal life out there. You can just cut to the chase with Carl and say yes."

"Carl is the icon of all players, pimps, and gangsters," stated Veronica. "He got older, and we all can see that his movies now evolved into the romance category. Every romance movie, he's

94

stripped naked and having sex. All of it worries me about dating him."

"It's only a movie," replied Ms. Cobblestone. "You have to differentiate acting from reality. You said he's out here filming. I would suggest going to the set to see for yourself to put your mind at ease. You've got to marry that man!"

"If I were ever to marry Carl, I feel that he'd cheat on me for sure. Plus, he'll never be home with all the filming he does. Women grab for him everywhere he goes! From where I stand, being who he is with ladies, I just don't know if I can trust a man like him."

"Why do you keep making it negative?" Ms. Cobblestone headed back to her office. "If he goes outside of a marriage, you sue his pants off and live off of a large settlement or hefty checks. Make sure not to sign any prenuptial, so there is no way he can screw you for his supposed mistakes. One false move of his and you could own this magazine company! I'm just looking out for you, honey. I sure wish I had what you've got in your hands: A goldmine!"

Chapter 8

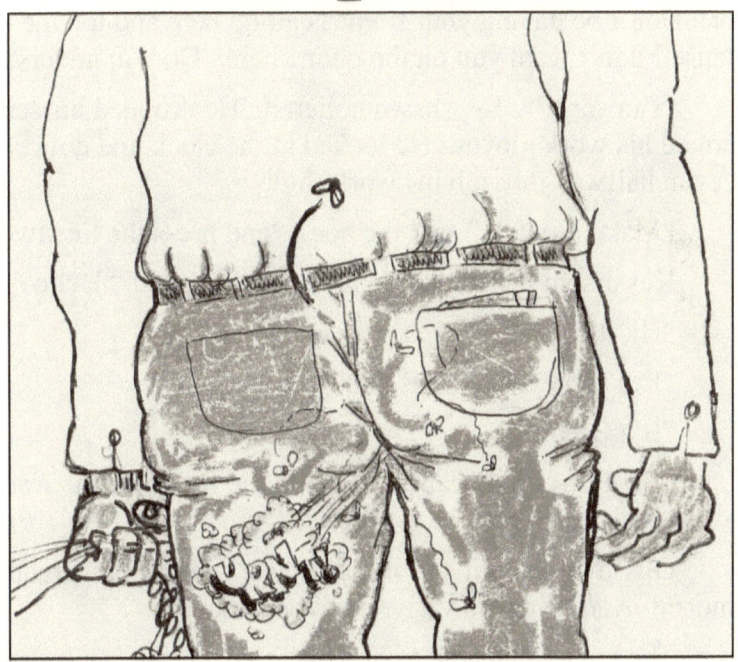

Something Stank

"Keyshawn, you have a call on line two! I told you about getting calls at work from your friends! The lady refused to get off the phone and tried to threaten me if I did not get you on the line."

Everybody heard the boss over the warehouse intercom.

"Veronica is going to end up getting you fired, bro." Vern shook his head at Keyshawn. "You'd better tell her off about calling you at work and then apologize to the boss. I can't be losing my best friend at work. Know what I'm saying?"

"It must be a hell of important for her to be calling me here," whispered Keyshawn. "Maybe Veronica wants to apologize?"

"Come get this phone, Keyshawn!" The boss shouted across his desk and waited to hear such a meaningful conversation. "I cannot be having my workers offline; we're in peak season! I need you on the floor! Don't be having your friends call up here and tell me off because I don't want you on the phone here. Do you understand?"

"I'm sorry!" Keyshawn hollered. He dropped his scanner and removed his work gloves. He looked at the clock and noticed he was not even halfway through his work shift.

"Make it quick," said the boss, "and press the line two."

Keyshawn picked up the phone and greeted, "Hello?"

"Hi, it's me!"

"I'm sorry, but who is this?"

"It's Olivia!"

The boss could hear her through the receiver; she was excitedly loud. He asked, "And who the fuck is Olivia?"

Olivia heard him and shouted, "He can call me Grand Camorra! And he doesn't have to be so nosey!"

The boss whispered to Keyshawn, "Did she say her name is Grand Camorra. Are you talking to that fine ass weather chick? Did you go from Veronica Evans to Grand Camorra? I'll be damned!"

Keyshawn tried to listen to Olivia, but the warehouse supervisors physically congratulated him with high fives and fist bumps. Suddenly, his frown grew into a marvelous smile as production stopped, and more workers gathered to listen to his call.

"How did you get my number at my work?"

"You were a little tipsy the other night when you told me where you work," she said. "I looked it up, and here we are."

"Cool. I'm glad that you called me, but my boss is very strict about us getting calls here. Would you mind if I called you back, like on a break?"

"He can't talk right now," said his boss. "He's at work, Grand Camorra. He can talk to you on his dime and at his cell."

"Your boss sounds like a prick," chuckled Olivia. "Listen, I just wanted to know if you'd like to hang out this evening. I'm sorry that I didn't get in touch with you sooner; I just returned to town after an audition in New York. My agent booked me without notice, and it appears that I may get the role. I wanted to make sure I spent time with my new friend before leaving for a bit of time. Perhaps we could have dinner later? If not tonight, maybe we can meet tomorrow for lunch, even?"

"Of course, we can meet tonight! I'm off at five."

"Okay, I'll let you go now, Keyshawn. After you get off, just come by the hotel on 3rd and Monroe, the Grand Arcs. I'm in room 69. I didn't want to meet at my home on the first date. I'm a little uncomfortable doing that, but anyway we can decide what to eat from there. And if you have any issues finding me, my temporary number is (310) 555-1212. Okay?"

"I got it."

"I have to run," said Olivia. "I have a little acting gig in about an hour. I might be at the hotel after six. Just wait for me if I'm late."

"You bet!"

Click. Keyshawn hung up and rapidly strutted back to his isle.

"See!" Vern nodded to Keyshawn. "I hooked you up at the club the other night by pointing her out. Who's the man, bro?"

"You were right," answered Keyshawn. "You're the man. It sounds like she's crazy about me too. This time, I got her number; I'm meeting her after work at a hotel."

"Keyshawn, you're the shit! Hey everybody, my man here is going out on another date with Grand Camorra! He's in there!"

All of the men and women nearby confusingly cheered and made him a national hero.

Vern added, "You make sure to watch for any cameras! You don't want your business on blast again."

"I honestly don't know what these famous chicks see in you," said Keyshawn's boss into the intercom, "but I'm giving you the rest of the shift off. I expect an autographed picture from Camorra for my generosity when you return to work!"

Another factory worker hollered, "Forget the autograph! Bring me back her panties!"

The crew cheered and carried on.

"Hey boss, I need to prepare him for how to handle this celebrity; you know, give him some pointers," said Vern.

The shift manager understood. "That would be smart. I know he fucked up with Veronica Evans. But if I let you go, I want an extra day worked this week from you. It's not even noon!"

"Thank you, sir!" Vern was excited. "If he plays his cards right with Grand Camorra, the benefits are great for us because she has plenty of friends. Know what I'm saying?"

"Now that's what I call looking out," replied the shift manager. Then he looked confused. "Too bad you can't get with any of her friends since you got a girlfriend."

Vern replied, "She'd better act right then."

A few minutes later, Keyshawn floored the metal to the pedal of his Cutlass towards Vern's home. As fast as he drove the car, it was almost a surprise that the cops didn't show up again. There were no cops in the vicinity. They were on the other side of town; they patrolled the film lot of Carl Cleveland and the movie crew.

"Cut!" cried the director. He was unhappy with the love scene on the public bench. The female fans could be heard for miles and made it known that they loved Carl and the actress. "You're going to need to give us more sexiness, Carl! No person is going to buy that!"

"I cannot focus out here," said Carl. "We should just film this steamy scene in the studio like you called for in the original script."

"No! No!" shouted the director. "The shot needs to be filmed out here on the park bench. Now, we can edit out the noises from the fans around here. What? Carl, you seem agitated."

"I cannot work with this local double," said Carl. He placed a towel around his waist. "I'm supposed to be doing a love scene with Shirley Love and not with this big boob tramp! I don't care if she's local. Why must we use a double? I want the real thing!"

"Who are you calling a tramp?" screamed the actress, who

100

bared no shame of her near nudity in public. "How dare you call me that? Do you know who I am? You're not all that, Carl! I read that you're dating Veronica Evans nowadays. I cannot believe any woman would want you; you smell like shit, and your acting stinks!"

The director angrily ordered the hired double to cover up and return to the clothing coordinator's trailer until he got things figured out. More than likely, the double was done with the casting call.

"You're not all that either!" Carl flipped off the double as she walked away. "Who hires an actress double that wears a damn cup in her panties during a love scene? We're not playing football, bitch! Go back to telling the weather on the local news and quit acting forever!"

"Look, Carl," the director pleaded, "you know that Shirley Love is now religious. She doesn't do sex scenes anymore. All I need for you to do is the act or do I need to find a double for you that can pull off the love scene?"

Carl furiously placed his hands on his hips. "Look, man, I know that I dragged us out here to California to film this, but I can find other projects to work with if this isn't going to work."

"No, please don't do that. I need you in this movie!"

"This is Los Angeles, and this is where movies are made," reminded Carl. "Shirley Love is in the mecca of actresses. We flew her from New York to act! She either does the love scene with me, or I walk and throw her reputation under the bus! With Shirley's years in the business, I'm sure that she'll understand to put aside her moral standards when it comes to keeping her status. I'm Carl Cleveland, and I do not do love scenes with doubles! She had better recognize!"

The director threw up his arms. He walked Carl into the converted studio set, which was previously an unleased warehouse. "Come on, Carl. You're a bit too stubborn for this project. Remember that I'm the director and producer! I tell you what works."

"If you want me at my best and to make something out of a crappy script, then you give me what I want for it to work! I've been in this business for a long time, so don't try and play me for a rookie. Movies are my game! I run this! Now, I told you what I want. Make some magic, or else!"

"Okay, fine!" The director stormed out of the studio to retrieve Shirley Love.

Nearly a half-hour later, Veronica Evans, accompanied by Carl's security, entered the studio. It was darkened inside, with a few soft lights centered within a circle of cameras. She could hear Carl Cleveland faintly talking, so she quietly sped up to see the scene being performed. She couldn't wait to see Carl perform with her own eyes.

"I paid you a hell of a lot of extra money to drop your newfound religious values, girl!" The director was angry. "Now you're going to have to drop your panties like you used to do in the '70s! Take it all off, Shirley! Yes, show us those classic jugs!"

Shirley reluctantly removed all of her clothing and recited to Carl, "I love you. I do. By gosh, I hope that you sincerely love me. I've never been with a man before, and I just want our love to be right. Take me now, honey. Take me!"

Carl Cleveland, stark naked, spun the old actress around and rammed into her spine with his abs. He whispered, "I'll take you, alright. I just have one thing to say before I smash your guts."

"What's that, you stud?"

"Two ripe, make the world go long because I don't see anything wrong with loving you all night. Give me your loving!"

"Oh, yes!" screamed Shirley Love. It'd been a while since she'd cried out in such artistic felony. She was driven up and down the dirty studio wall, as sweat splattered between her and Carl. "Oh, my goodness, baby, take me! That's what I need!"

Carl pounded his dark hips into Shirley's flabby, pale backside as if somebody repeatedly poked his buttocks with a needle.

Unfortunately for Veronica, unnoticed by any of the production crew, the raunchy sex scene looked and sounded all too real. She didn't like the way Shirley Love gasped and howled like mad. She didn't like the sweat pouring off the edge of Carl's bare butt or the moving shadows between his grapefruits and the wall. Disgusted, Veronica was turned off with Carl.

Carl flipped the old actress around and kneaded her aged breasts with his hands. She seemed to enjoy every part of the scene.

"Uh!" hollered the actress, as she was roughly folded and hammered from wall to wall. She could hardly catch her breath.

Veronica turned around and hostilely walked out of the studio. That's when Carl heard the squeaky studio door and saw the light.

"Veronica?" Carl ended the act. "No! Oh, man."

Shirley covered up. "What are you doing, Carl? We're not finished! You get back over here, you stud!"

The director stood up from his chair. "What do you mean, *oh, no*? Carl, we have a scene to finish! Where are you going?"

"I'll be back. Just hold on a second!" Carl placed on a robe and dashed out of the studio. He caught up to Veronica.

"I saw you in there," she angrily stated. "That was real sex!"

"No, it wasn't," he replied. "I'm an actor. Remember? We have to sell the crowd on it being real!"

"I know what I saw! How could you with an 80-year-old?"

"I'm no porn star," chuckled Carl. "Neither is Shirley Love. We are actors, and that's all you witnessed!"

"Why do you smell like sex, then?"

"We get excited," answered Carl. "Our body fluids sometimes leaks out. I assure you that we did not have sex; I've been straight with you since we met. It's only acting; I'm playing a rough villain in this movie, so it involves a rough sex scene. I wish I had known ahead of time that you were dropping by. I could've given you a heads up."

"It just looked too real; I didn't like it!"

"So, you don't like rated R movies? That's all it is."

"I'm not saying that," answered Veronica. "You know what? I'm tripping. You're only doing your job. I'm sorry. You're right that I should've let you know I was coming to the set."

"We're just two older actors and actresses in there trying to sell into the younger movie-goer demographic; it has to look real," explained Carl. He walked back into the studio. "It's only a movie, Veronica. Just wait for me out here. The love scene, with breaks, should be longer than ten minutes. I'll be right back!"

Veronica was speechless. After all, she's the one that agreed to date a man that was notorious for making out in romance movies like that. Did Veronica plan to change him? She knew that she couldn't do a thing about his job. If she wanted to stay with such a sex symbol from movies, she had to just deal with it.

Carl closed the studio door behind. "That was a close one," he thought to himself and swallowed.

But what he found next in the studio was that it was closed and production shut down for the day. "Where'd everybody go?"

The entire production crew left for the day out the front door, except for Shirley and the director. He had Shelly Love's head dribbling against the boom microphone above, while he made vicious loving to her throughout the bedroom set. She battled to keep from swallowing her dentures and losing her wig.

"I quit!" shouted Carl. He walked out of there, angry as ever.

"What happened in there?" asked Veronica. "Why are you so upset? I thought you said the scene would be ten minutes or so?"

"I just want to get my clothing out of the trailer, and we can be on our way for dinner, perhaps."

"That sounds good to me, Carl."

Together, they walked around a couple of corners and came upon Carl's trailer.

"Why does it smell like dirty drawers around here?"

"My bodyguards are probably inside enjoying some chitterlings they got from the best chicken joint downtown."

"There's no way I'm going inside your trailer! I cannot stand the way those taste!"

Carl replied, "Let me run inside and clean up. I promise that I won't be very long. I will just be in and out."

He opened his trailer door and found that one of his bodyguards quietly did the do with an oddly familiar woman. She was supposed to do an exclusive interview with Shirley Love after today's production. There wasn't a trace of chitterlings inside the trailer. Carl closed and locked the door. He gestured for them to keep it down because Veronica was outside. Then he turned up heavy metal music that rattled the trailer and got him some!

Veronica went ahead and waited for nearly ten to fifteen minutes, which seemed like an eternity. However, when Carl exited the trailer, accompanied by one of his bodyguards, he was showered, dressed in a costly suit, and smelled wonderful. His attitude was much more relaxed now.

"Do you always take a shower with the music that loud? And were you dancing in there? The shocks on the mobile home squeaked like crazy! I thought the wheels would fall off."

One of Carl's bodyguards looked at him and smirked.

Carl responded to Veronica. "Yeah, I like music. We were rocking it in there. I like to dance in the shower. Shall we go now?"

After another thirty minutes, Carl's limousine pulled upfront to an Italian restaurant. When they entered, a generous waiter seated them both, while Carl's bodyguard sat over at the restaurant bar.

"It is a pleasure to serve you both this evening," greeted their waiter. He was indeed star-struck as he handed them their menus. "Welcome. I hope that you find our seating exquisite to your liking. May I start either of you off with one of our finest wines tonight or an appetizer?"

Carl answered, "Thank you. My taste buds are up for a little wine. I'll take your finest."

"Of course," answered the waiter. "I will bring that to you. And what shall I bring for the stunning Veronica Evans?"

"You're too much," chuckled Veronica. "I think that I'll just have a light beer."

The waiter continued. "That will be very well, ma'am. Please, you both take your time looking over the menu. I will be your server tonight. My name is Ricardo Bianchi."

"Thank you," replied Veronica. She watched the waiter walk away and wondered why she had never eaten at this restaurant. It was very hospitable and romantic.

"You know, it's refreshing to be with here with you." Carl

tilted his head and looked into Veronica's eyes. "You bring the best out of me. You know, I'm wondering if there's kind of something between you and me by now."

"You're straight to the point. I like that in a man, Carl."

"We're both celebrities, and you know how time can be with our deadlines and all."

"That's so true."

Carl honestly asked, "So, have you been able to close the deal with the ex-boyfriend? I don't want to step in the middle of anything like we had at your job that one morning."

Veronica giggled. "Trust me when I say that I have moved on from him. He's done."

"As beautiful as you are, it's hard to imagine he would be."

"Well, believe it."

"It's impossible. You're the greatest!"

"I'm not greater than Grand Camorra."

"Trust me, Veronica. I know of her, and she's nothing but a fill-in actress and a skanky whore. Your ex-boyfriend is settling for someone who will never be exclusively his. You have to trust me on that, being straight to the point."

"She's all over the place, eh?"

"I wouldn't say that," he replied. "Grand Camorra, from what I heard, doesn't do intercourse with any men. She satisfies, though."

"And you'd know that how?"

"In this business," answered Carl, "actors share insider secrets. You're a journalist; maybe you can interview her one day. All I can say I heard is that her lips are her greatest asset, and the buck stops there from stories I've heard from my constituents."

"It is amazing, considered the body she has."

"So Veronica... since this is a date, can we consider us a couple? I think that you're marvelous!"

"I don't know," replied Veronica. "I mean, don't get it twisted, as if I don't like you, Carl. For me, before I settle into a relationship, I like to test everything first. Allow me to get to know all of you. How can we be great lovers, if we can't be great friends first?"

For the next hour, the two hit it off pretty well and got to know each other. It turned out that Carl and Veronica had a bit in common, being adopted out east as children to white parents. Soundly in love with each other also, they opened up a lot of heart-filled subjects.

After a lovely dinner, Carl and Veronica rode the limousine back to the movie production trailers.

"Well, let's do it again soon." Carl walked Veronica to her car.

Veronica moved her bangs and asked, "Carl, it is still kind of early in the night, so would you like to maybe come by my place and have dessert tonight? We could order a movie on television."

"I wouldn't want to impose."

"I'd like you to come over and stay the night."

Veronica gave Carl her home number and address. Carl gave the note to his bodyguard.

"This is a night for only you and me," said Veronica. "He is not invited. Why are you giving my information to him?"

"My bodyguards are always close to me because some fans are out of their minds."

"I'm not a fan, and my mind is clear."

"You do know that I'm legendary in movies," said Carl, "so my bodyguards are always near. They can wait outside."

Veronica respected that.

"Just for a little while, I guess I can stop by." Carl sat in Veronica's car. She drove away, as Carl's bodyguards followed in a black limousine.

"Just scoot the seat back if you're out of leg space," said Veronica. "As you can see, my ex had short legs like a troll."

Soon enough, they reached their destination: Veronica's home.

"This is a nice house," stated Carl.

Once inside, Veronica took Carl's coat and left for her bedroom. "Carl, I need to freshen up a bit. Just make yourself at home, and I'll be right out. There are few bottles of wine in the refrigerator if you want a little more to drink tonight."

Carl knew what the night was about, so he prayed that he could still perform. He swallowed a blue pill because, after all, he had sex with multiple women in the last two days. He just felt that Veronica wasn't entirely over Keyshawn, so she was going to be reckless about revenge over Grand Camorra.

"I am the man even thirty years after my acting began! I'm nearly averaging what I did back then!" Carl thought.

Blup-blup-blup-Ee-errr! His stomach growled. Carl had to get rid of that bubbly air and creamy pasta dinner from his system as soon as possible. The dinner had not agreed with him. He silently farted mustard and stood from the couch. He hustled to the hallway bathroom and flicked the toilet lid up. As he sat towards the toilet seat, the toilet lid bounced off the toilet tank and back onto the toilet seat. Carl sat upon the toilet lid and realized it was too late! He spilled diarrhea over the toilet lid.

"Oh damn it to hell!"

Veronica returned to the living room and turned on her stereo to soulful slow jams. Carl returned to the living room with welts of sweat hanging from his forehead. He did the best he could do with cleaning up the toilet and rug in the bathroom.

"Are you okay, Carl? You look bothered." Veronica strolled towards him, wearing only shoe-string strips of red, silky gown and panties that left nothing to secrecy. Her skin was oiled with Brazilian cocoa butter and drizzled with London's lavish.

Carl licked his lips at the fullness of her breasts and the roundness of her hips. She had long legs, like helicopter blades, as strong as a stallion. He pulled his pants off and tossed his dirty draws into her Lemon Lime Dracaena! "Veronica, you look stunning tonight. Let's get to this, sugar."

"I think I'm in love with you, Carl."

"I know you are," he responded. "You can't hide that from me. Come here and get down on your knees."

Veronica surrendered to his desire and knelt between his legs.

She placed a hand on both of his thighs and massaged him into his waxed nature. She certainly enjoyed her hair being stroked by Carl's soft hands as she paused before invading his jewels.

"Do you love me, Veronica? I want to hear you say it!"

"I love you, Carl."

"Show me how much you love me, honey!"

Carl shuffled around on the beige couch, as his stomach still ailed from the creamy white sauce with broccoli and pasta dinner he ate earlier. He could not get comfortable enough to enjoy Veronica's lips that pecked from one of his knees to his thigh. It felt so good that Carl tightened his abs and held in farts. He wanted to get even more comfortable for what was to come!

So, he shifted into a position that left his back on the couch and his butt exposed to air. That's when Veronica inhaled and snorted up the most dastardly funk, a doo-doo smell that one would find on the ground in front of a heavily used portable toilet from somebody that didn't make it in time at a chili cookout.

"What in the hell is that awful smell, Carl?"

"What smell? I don't smell anything! Keep going. You're almost there, just a few more inches."

Veronica chucked up a little wine and noodles from the dinner earlier. "Man, you better stand your nasty ass up from my couch!"

Both Carl and Veronica stood and saw the damage to the couch. It wasn't a beached whale in perspective, but Carl left a beached trout and an oil spill on the end of her couch.

"I'm going to be so freaking sick!" declared Veronica. "You shit on my couch! You need to go see a doctor, man!"

"I did not do that! That stain was already there. I thought it was from a long time ago or something. Maybe, your ex did that?"

"Why don't you explain that awful smell, man?"

"I thought it was just the smell of your house!"

"What? Are you trying to say that my house smells like shit?" Veronica was a hell of mad. "Is that what you're saying?"

"Maybe it is what I'm saying!"

Veronica surprisingly shoved Carl onto the couch. When he stood back up, there was another new, liquidly brown streak on her couch that matched his hairy butt crack!

Veronica asked herself, "Where's my gun? Carl, you'd better clean that shit off my couch now! I mean it!"

"I'm sorry. I really am. I get the leaks!"

"Go into the kitchen and grab some napkins! There are cleaning supplies underneath the sink! Do you not know how to clean your ass after you take a shit? Oh my word, you're so disgusting!"

Minutes later, Carl swept the remaining dried pebbles of his feces into a napkin with his hands. "Did I get it all? I think that's it. Veronica, I'm so sorry about those streaks on your couch. What do you want me to do with these toothbrushes I used to clean the couch?"

"You get the hell... out of my house!" Veronica booked to the kitchen sink and puked her guts out! "Leave here! If I didn't know the Lord, I'd...! Just, get your stank ass out of my house, brah'!"

"I thought you said you loved me, Veronica. Most men my age have these kinds of problems. It's normal, girl!"

"Get the hell out of my house, you disgusting sicko!"

Carl expeditiously left Veronica's house. He knew that if he wanted her, he would have to work harder than ever before. He stained that off-white couch for life, along with, perhaps his celebrity image. Carl may have destroyed his reputation if any of his date with Veronica got out to the public. On top of everything else, she had to be a celebrity gossip journalist.

Sometimes, Love Just Won't Let Go

By Ashaki Boelter

Chapter 9

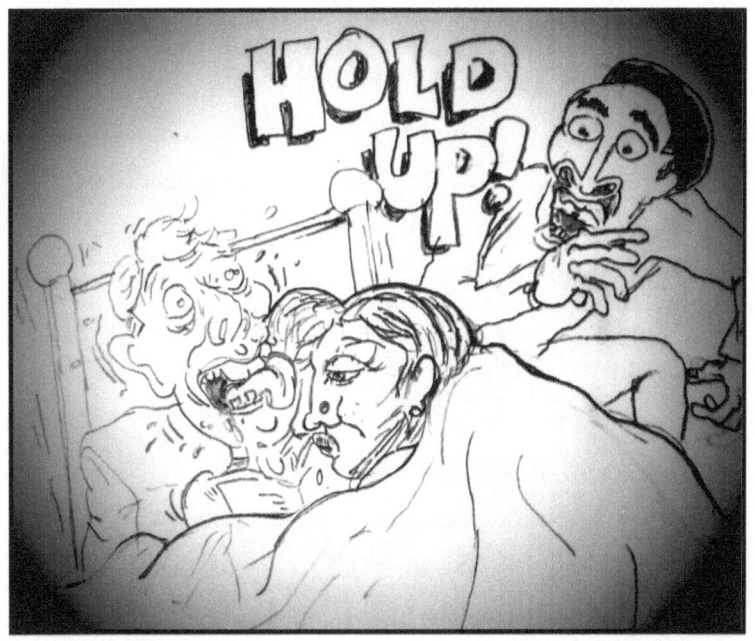

Bumping and Grinding

"So, did you get some last night? Keyshawn, wake up!"

"Vern, I'm not telling you anything. The whole world wants to be up in my business. How late did I sleep in?"

"It's like ten in the morning!" Vern giggled. "My boy did-the-do, and it wore you the hell out! Good for you! Know what I'm saying? I'm glad that you took my advice after work. But I hope it was better than Veronica's experience with Carl Cleveland. Know what I'm saying? She, at least, made the paper."

"Whatever dude. What are you talking about now?"

"According to the paper this morning, right on the front of the Entertainment section here, it shows Veronica going to a fancy Italian

113

restaurant on the other side of town with Carl. You don't want to read the article because they went to her home afterward. Know what I'm saying? Yeah, Veronica got some Carl salami!"

"We just went to dinner."

"You didn't get some poontang?"

"Grand Camorra and I had a nice dinner and talked."

"Well, it's no wonder you didn't make headlines, Keyshawn!"

"Man, don't do that, Vern!"

"Do what?"

"And I don't want to hear about Veronica's every move. She can do whatever she wants. I don't care anymore about her."

"That's my boy!" Then a tear dropped from Vern's right eye.

"Vern, what was that? I saw that!"

"It was nothing. Know what I'm saying?"

"You're crying! Vern, what's up with the tears?"

Vern looked away to hide his pain and his foretold shame. "Rochelle left me last night, dude. Know what I'm saying?"

"What? Man, I'm sorry. What happened?"

Vern mumbled words and ended his unrecognized sentence with *La Donna.*

"All I heard was *La Donna.* Man, what happened?"

"Okay, man," answered Vern. "After you left for your date, La Donna just happened to come to my door, giving church tracts. The art intrigued me, and then it straight up scared me about going to hell. Know what I'm saying? You know how I am with scary stuff. I can't believe churches hand those out to little kids! Plus, it was getting dark outside, and Rochelle was still at work for a few more hours."

"Please, tell me that you didn't invite her inside."

"I invited her in because she needed a cup of water from doing all that talking about salvation throughout our neighborhood. So, I invited her inside for a drink of water. She was modestly dressed and seemed religious. I'll tell you what, though. Even in a long dress to her feet, all that sweaty material stuck to every inch of her booty! I thought it was sexy to see her panty lines. I could see every jiggle she made when she walked, right through modesty!"

"It was probably dumb to let her in the house. And we agreed that there were no chicks allowed in here too."

"You are correct!" Vern agreed. "But, it's originally my place, and I make changes when necessary to the rules.

"Oh, okay."

"I had La Donna up in here, so…" Vern continued. "When I opened the fridge to get out the ice water, she saw all the alcohol and went crazy! She shoved me out of the way and just started drinking from the bottles! Know what I'm saying? She kept on asking for God's forgiveness after each bottle. I thought all of it was sexy! Then she got drunk and transformed into a super freak! I ain't lying!"

"Here we go."

"Keyshawn, I couldn't keep her hands off of me!" Vern gulped. "I had to surrender! Know what I'm saying? She tore off her dress like a superheroine and carried me to my bedroom. She was like, bionic and milked me like a chocolate cow! Know what I'm saying? We had intergalactic supernova sex!"

"Man, you're an idiot! How did Rochelle find out?"

"Rochelle came to my house and caught us in bed. I guess that I forgot to lock the front door."

"And you're still living?"

"Shit, I hid behind La Donna." Vern was proud. "Rochelle beat the living hell out of La Donna using a cast-iron skillet! La Donna didn't have any clothes on and ran out the door and down the street. I think that she called rideshare to get her home."

"Damn!"

"La Donna will never sleep with me again, and Rochelle is gone for good. Know what I'm saying? That hurts down deep, man."

"I tried to warn you that this would happen!"

"What's messed up, though, besides the crabs that I ended up getting from La Donna, is that I can't afford this apartment anymore.

115

Rochelle paid half of the rent since she stayed here more than she did at her parents' house."

"So, what are you going to do?"

"You mean, what are *you* going to do? Keyshawn, you don't have a place to call home either unless you start paying part of the rent here. This isn't a homeless shelter, homeboy. Know what I'm saying? You're picking up her portion of the rent starting next week. That should teach you not to move into a bitch's house so fast, out of love, as you did with Veronica. She made you homeless when she dumped you, but luckily, you got a friend like me."

"Well, that will give me half the ownership of this apartment than right?"

"I guess."

"Well, Vern, I am asking you to give me a little privacy this afternoon. I have my guest coming by to pick me up for lunch, but now that I live here, we'll do lunch here. I'll even let you borrow my Cutlass for a bit so that you can leave. Just be responsible."

Vern was like, "Is it Grand Camorra? Why can't I be here to meet her? Oh man, you have to introduce me to her before you do her! Know what I'm saying? She can hook me up with her friends!"

"Just give me a couple of hours with her alone. I'll ask her about any available friends for you."

"That's my boy!"

"This place is a mess. Do you think we could straighten it up a little? You want her to get a good idea of how clean you are. Can you imagine her telling her friends how great you are, if your house is trash? I doubt she'd even put your name out there."

"Yeah, I guess it is a little messed up after the fight last night." Vern pointed out how the furniture was out of place and how dust-covered some of the furniture. "Why don't you go drive to the store and get the stuff to make her a dynamite lunch, while I clean up the place. It won't take me but thirty minutes to an hour. When you come back, I should just be leaving."

"That sounds good to me, Vern."

116

So, Keyshawn walked out of the front door with his wallet and keys. He got into his Cutlass and drove away to the national supermarket chain with the slowest cashiers on the planet.

"Well," whispered Vern, as he closed the kitchen curtain, "now that Keyshawn is gone for a minute, it is time to go to work. I'm going to be rich! All of this will make for one great sex tape!"

The horny friend walked to the rear of his duplex, opened the backyard patio door, walked into the small backyard, and looked at his stacks of 66-quart storage boxes under the roof. He moved a few of them to get to the bottom ones. Inside those boxes were CD-R disks of women he recorded while forking, and a variety of spy cameras.

"Yeah, boy," said Vern, "I'll be making a grip on auction sites after today, selling Grand Camorra's Sex Scandal video!"

The dirty dog strutted into his duplex and set up all the wireless spy cameras, throughout. He planted them behind pictures, in the filthy laundry, and even in the rusty toilet!

Within minutes of Vern planting the final spy camera in a plant and pushing record on his hidden laptop, which he plugged in, Keyshawn walked into the duplex.

"Man, the kitchen still looks a mess!" shouted Keyshawn. "It still smells a little bad in here. We need to open the windows! What have you been doing all this time? It doesn't look like you lifted a finger!"

"I was in the john," answered Vern. "If you need to know, I have a bad stomach from all this stress. Know what I'm saying? I'm sorry, man. Hey, Key, don't let this ruin our friendship or my meeting any of Grand Camorra's friends."

"Okay then, be quick about cleaning up in here! I called her, and she'll be here in about thirty minutes. I need to start cooking."

"I got it handled Key. I won't ruin your date today. I'll put clean sheets on my bed so that you and your gal can get it on! Know what I'm saying? Just tell her that my room is your room."

"I don't expect we'll be going that far. I am still trying to get to know Olivia. I don't want anything complicated."

"You *have* to go that far!" demanded Vern. He wasn't going to

117

hear that. "Chicks like her want it all the time, and you need to wipe Veronica out of your soul completely! Know what I'm saying? You never forget ho's fast enough, like Veronica, unless the getting is good! And just so you know, there are handcuffs underneath the right-side pillow of the bed and a battery-operated vibrator under the other."

For the next twenty minutes, Keyshawn cooked a wonderful lunch, and Vern cleaned up.

"It smells good in here," said Vern. "What is that, buffalo chicken wings? You made some yams and some collard greens. Oh, yeah, let me get one of those flaky biscuits, and I'll be on my way."

"Thanks for cleaning up the place."

"No worries. Well, I'd better be going. Grand Camorra should be getting here any minute."

"Why are you going out the back door?"

Vern stopped in his tracks. That part of the plan, he had forgotten to orchestrate effectively. He only had Wi-Fi for his laptop at home and not in the car, so he planned to be in his backyard the entire time, with some of his neighborly chums and watching.

"I don't know what I'm thinking." Vern chuckled. He grabbed Keyshawn's car keys and headed out the front door. "Hey, I'll see you later. Have a good time! You earned it by now, bro."

The thug strutted out the front door, got in Keyshawn's ride, and peeled out around the corner. He parked the car in front of a house and sprinted back to his backyard. He hopped the fence without Keyshawn or any of his friends' wives noticing from their homes. He landed behind the bushes and then high-fived his homeboys.

After he collected admission prices, Vern dodged and flipped to the deck and pulled his fully charged laptop from the wall, and rejoined the rest of his pals in the bushes.

"Let the show begin!"

"A big limousine just pulled up in front of your place," declared one of the dirty men from work. "Grand Camorra should be walking in that door any minute. I cannot wait to see that ass of hers!"

Meanwhile, back inside Vern's duplex, Keyshawn opened the

front door to let Olivia, also known as Grand Camorra, inside.

"It smells so good in here," said Olivia. "Thanks for inviting me over for lunch. I just happened to get another acting gig, so I don't have all but a couple of hours here."

Olivia badly wanted to tell Keyshawn of her previous gig with Carl Cleveland, but she did not want to ruin anything. She could tell that Keyshawn was a little hurt from breaking up with Veronica. Olivia stayed away from all that.

"Perhaps you could come with me to the studio and watch my performance, Keyshawn?"

"I would love to see you act!"

Outside in the back, a bunch of men smacked their lips with disdain. "Man, as slow as they're moving to fix their plate, they won't have time to get busy. Man, this is going to be a bust and a waste of time. We want our money back."

"What?" Vern tried to calm everyone down. "Don't worry! My dude is horny for her. He's going to hit that booty any second!"

Yet, to Vern's incredible might to read his closest friend, Keyshawn and Olivia left without doing a damn thing.

The two lovers simply ate lunch and got on their way to Olivia's film location.

"Hello, everyone," greeted Olivia. "This is my friend Keyshawn. He'll be watching me act today. I hope I wasn't too late. My driver forgot to get some change for the toll payment. Luckily, Keyshawn had a little change on him after he went to the store."

"He's kind of cute," said another actress. "He's a lot cuter in person than on that police show."

Keyshawn blushed.

"Yeah, I think so too." Olivia kissed Keyshawn on his sweaty forehead. "He cooked me lunch and everything today."

The entire camera crew was impressed. The director walked up to Keyshawn and looked into his eyes. He asked Olivia, "Eh, are you sure he should be here? He doesn't look like the type who could comprehend or appreciate finer arts."

119

Olivia answered, "He's a good and understanding man. He'll love it. If you want me at my best, you want him nearby to inspire me! I'm sure that he can handle a love scene."

"Of course, I can," replied Keyshawn.

"Eh, whatever works, darling," said the director. "Let us get started, as time is money. Thank you for responding, in short notice, Grand Camorra. I wouldn't want anyone else substituted for the scene beside you. Now, please get into your wardrobe and meet at Stage B… Please, be there in ten! Chop - chop!"

Olivia blew Keyshawn a kiss and walked away to prepare for the steamy role. Keyshawn and the unsure director walked over to Stage B. They took a seat. The director didn't say a word to him, as they both looked over the set that looked like a sultry bedroom.

Within minutes, the desired actress, Grand Camorra strolled onto Stage B in white, silky lingerie. Confident, in control, and sexy, she puckered her lips with attitude and flared her nostrils. Her eyes fixed on the bed upon the set, as if she wanted to grind across it as if it were the desired human. Grand Camorra awaited the director's cue.

"You look marvelous, honey!" shouted the director. He had always admired Grand Camorra's gorgeous, bodacious, and chiseled body. Then he turned to Keyshawn. "You are a lucky man. A lot of men would like, so' kill to be with that one, dear."

"Thanks." Grand Camorra wanted to show the world that she was ready for more prominent roles, and thanks to Carl Cleveland's insults during the last audition, she was going to put her all into this opportunity.

"Okay!" shouted the director. "Everybody take your place! Turn on the red lights! Let's make history, girls! Now roll it!"

An ailing man crawled into a bed and acted as if his life was terminal. He groaned, "Oh, fairy godmother, I have one wish left. I just want one incredible night of sex before I die! Oh, fairy godmother, where art thou? Grant me my third and final wish, oh godmother! If I die during sex, let it be. If I'm going to die, allow me to go with a smile."

"What the hell is this, a porno?" Keyshawn thought.

By Ashaki Boelter

Suddenly, the bedroom door opened, and Grand Camorra strolled towards the ailing actor. "I shall grant you thou wish, you naughty man." Then Grand Camorra seductively climbed onto the bed with her red heels on and crawled underneath the bed covers!

"Holy smokes!" hollered Keyshawn. He chuckled away like a little kid seeing a naked nudie for the first time. That scene turned him on; he wanted to fork the actress tonight!

"Shush!" warned the director. "I like what I see! Somebody say, *Oscar*! The loving is brilliant and awesome!"

Keyshawn stood up from the chair, as Grand Camorra went wild under the covers with the actor!

"Sit down, darling," said the director. "It's only soft porn, I promise you. They're not doing much. They're just bumping and grinding with a little groping. The editors will take out most of what they're doing to keep things cable ready, but don't forget to buy the unrated version when it comes out."

"Wow!" Keyshawn had never seen Grand Camorra like that in any movie! He heard the sensational sounds from their mouths and constant squeaking of the bed. The lights flickered above.

The scene ran a little long to Keyshawn's taste. He began to wonder how long the scene was going to last. His love interest was not going to have energy left for him later on; she'll be worn out! He could hear the soreness in her vocal, as both actors sounded like starting chain saws and donut-spinning automobiles.

"I can see the look on your face," said the director to Keyshawn. "There is a lot involved in a love scene, so be patient. We'll have your Grand Camorra out of there in minutes."

Keyshawn grew a little annoyed, nearly sickened. Something did not sound right under those sheets for just acting.

The director shouted, "We need to finish strong guys! Tear the roof off of the studio! Give me more! Let it fly!"

Suddenly, both stage presences hollered and whimpered!

"Cut!" shouted the director. "That's a masterpiece and wrap! Honey, you guys were terrific! It was so good that I almost exploded over your little friend here sitting next to me, Grand Camorra." He

121

began to laugh at his sense of humor.

"Fuck that!" Keyshawn jumped from his chair. "Man, you don't know me like that! You better check yourself. I ain't the one!"

The director smacked his lips. "Ewe, no, Grand Camorra, can you please take your feisty little friend away now? He seems to have an attitude problem. You may not want to bring him to your sets before exactly explaining what's going on. That's just some advice."

The actor, who enjoyed Olivia's sensuality under the covers, rumbled from under the sheets on the bed. He had no idea what had hit him! "That was some of the best sensual actings ever! Whoa!"

Keyshawn walked Olivia out of that studio. He watched her wipe away at her mouth. He asked, "You were acting, right?"

Olivia grabbed onto Keyshawn's hand. "Of course, we were acting, honey. Quit worrying. Did you enjoy it?"

"Yeah, I guess it was pretty sexy," Keyshawn added. "I've read a lot of sexual foul stuff about behind the scenes in movies, so just be straight with me."

Olivia sinisterly smirked at his command, but Keyshawn did not catch that.

By Ashaki Boelter

Chapter 10

Calling Me a Whore?

"**Y**ou have got to keep Carl Cleveland," advised Ms. Cobblestone. Her smiley face was more than devious; it was dirty. "That stud is so perfect for you, Veronica!"

"You don't even know him to say that!" Veronica was fed up with everybody that consistently said how great it was for her to be with one of the top actors of all time. As far as she was concerned, he humped actresses on the set, and in the process, he had broken something in his body so severely that he no longer had control of his ass muscles. Without those muscles, he couldn't hold his shit in anymore.

Sure. Carl was a gentleman, but Veronica had spent the last couple of nights disinfecting her couch. All she could think about was that she didn't want to get tied down to an older man that had those issues. To hell with doing that kind of laundry every!

"Why are you so disappointed in him? Veronica, if I had Carl, I'd be on cloud nine! You are truly blessed!"

"I am truly blessed?" All she could think about was Keyshawn because sometimes, love just wouldn't let go."

"All the money you're tied into with Carl," replied Ms. Cobblestone. "And he won't be all up in your face all the time, so you can still work, travel, and have a little fun. Those are great benefits!"

"I think he's already cheating on me."

"How do you know?"

"I just know."

"Well, let him cheat. That's all good. I told you that before!"

"What are you talking about, Ms. Cobblestone?"

"Marry him, bust him, and then sue his pants off! Remember?" Ms. Cobblestone clapped in pure delight. "There's not a woman on the planet that doesn't like him."

"It sounds as if you want to set him up."

"Dear no! I just want you to be happy."

"Do you want me to be happy with Carl or his money?"

Ms. Cobblestone thought for a second. It wasn't as if she did not know that messing with powerful men got her places. After all, She became powerful at She's Golden by walking in on the owner, Mr. Franklin, atop his desk with his front end inside the back end of a desperate mail clerk. Ms. Cobblestone was instantly offered her lucrative position by way of blackmail.

"You are crazy, boss. I am just not that scandalous."

"Oh, okay."

"I'm just not feeling Carl Cleveland."

"Oh, I see what's going on. You haven't fucked Carl yet."

"What does that have to do with anything?"

"I've heard about him. He's had *that* operation!"

By Ashaki Boelter

"Well, they should have inserted a permanent car fragrance up his ass with that operation. He cannot hold his shit in."

"You're worried about his some booty scent?" Ms. Cobblestone nodded. "I get it. Well, sometimes men don't use wet wipes after pooping or practicing, and the smells seep for days, especially when they're sweating. You have got to learn to plug your nose; I thought you'd have for sure learned that when you dated that baseball player. We are talking about Carl Cleveland for goodness sakes, so you need to make sacrifices!"

"I'm just not like you when it comes to getting screwed. I'm genuine, while you'd probably be willing to wear a bag over your head if a man asked you to."

"Are you calling me a whore?" Ms. Cobblestone took offense to Veronica's statement. "No, you didn't. At least I wasn't with a thug, who couldn't do squat except to hold you down from your full potential in life, generally speaking, and literally."

"How do you know? You weren't there!"

"With all that complaining and bashing you were doing about Keyshawn around here, you put us there. Did you say that bills were barely paid on time, he hangs around thugs that you refuse to have on your property, he couldn't keep a job, he couldn't stand the fact that you don't cook, and that your parents weren't into him? Since you started dating him, well after the initial week, you bashed him for something. Veronica, you've got a great man in Carl Cleveland, and he's the step in the only direction."

"Maybe I did say too much around here about Keyshawn's faults," said Veronica. She pulled her bangs back behind her ear. "Keyshawn wasn't that bad. I just wanted to make excuses for my shortcomings. All of you around here have got it wrong about him. I've realized that Keyshawn loved me the best way he could. It took me losing him and being with Carl to realize what I had."

"What are you saying, Veronica? Are you convincing yourself to reunite with that thug again? You'd be crazy to go back to Keyshawn! He's a loser! You are so happy with Carl! Will the real Veronica return to earth?"

The women around the office tuned in, as everyone could hear

125

the conversation. Many of the staff pulled out their pads to cover the story of possibly the end of Veronica Evan's career at She's Golden.

"I have shared with all of you in this office about my love life. Frankly, all of your advice has made things worse for me! I don't know why I listen to any of you!"

"It's because we're wise," said Ms. Cobblestone. Other coworkers verbally agreed, as if it were a church sermon. "We're all one big family, and we're all watching each other's back so we can continue to produce the greatest gossip magazine in the nation."

"I bet most of you here have problems of your own in your relationships because of bad advice floating around here."

"Now, don't turn this on us!" Ms. Cobblestone sternly spoke and stood up, high and mighty. "The bottom line is that you talk too damn much about your business in a place where our opinions and creativity make and break celebrities. It's on you that we're all in your business, big mouth! It sounds as if you're broken."

"I talk too much?"

All of the coworkers responded, "Yes!"

A coworker said, "We know Keyshawn's shoe size, where he's from, his favorite television shows, his grandmother's name, and his pants size. We know he has a tiny tattoo above his belly button."

Another coworker added, "We know his driver's license number, his high school prom date's last name, and what he likes for foreplay!"

One more coworker stepped up. "Veronica, we all know what his favorite toothpaste is and about the brand and size of contraceptives he likes to use. You even told us one day that he used only his tongue to get you to…"

"Okay! Okay!" interrupted Veronica.

Ms. Cobblestone raised her shoulders. "I told you so. *You have a big mouth.* So, don't expect any sympathy from me right now. We saw what was best and gave you great advice. So, you stick to Carl because he is the right kind of man for you. I know you. And don't forget about the ultimatum I'd given you. I can't be having you jeopardize the integrity of this company by sleeping around with a black criminal, gangster thug that can't even pronounce words correctly, and carries drugs everywhere he goes! For all you know, he could be hiding all kinds of stuff from you, if not a disease. And last but not least, where was he headed the night he got pulled over?"

"I can't believe you said all of that about somebody you don't even know. Besides, Police Tales is a television show, which is sometimes scripted. He could've just been a victim of circumstance."

Ms. Cobblestone obnoxiously laughed.

"Veronica, she's right," said a coworker. "Ms. Cobblestone has a point. I once dated a thug, and he gave me herpes."

Devon, the blushed, red-headed Caucasian, added, "Veronica, I'm sorry but… Keyshawn is a gorilla."

Ms. Cobblestone stopped laughing. The entire staff stopped.

"You just called Keyshawn a gorilla?" Veronica snapped. She removed her earrings and started to pull her hair back into a bun. "See, white boy, you just fucked up with that comment. I may be the only sister in this office, but I am not going to tolerate that!"

Devon unsurely chuckled and fixed his tie. However, it was fate or just coincidence that the owner of She's Golden entered the office. He was baffled that he hadn't been made aware of the meeting.

Devon spouted, "We just disagree, sir."

"I'll take care of this, everybody." Ms. Cobblestone immediately grabbed Veronica's arm and dragged her off into her office and closed the door. "Get in here, now! What in the hell is wrong with you? There are better ways to handle racist comments. I'll deal with Devon. That was not okay."

Veronica stood there, as Ms. Cobblestone pulled the shades to the windows to her office. They now had privacy.

"I don't know what has crawled into your panties," said Ms. Cobblestone, "but that was uncalled for! We don't threaten our team members; we're a family. Now, you're a great journalist, and everybody knows that. I would never want to fire you over retaliation of something right. I need you here! We are girls, Veronica! Now, I'll fix whatever was broken with that threat I am sure Mr. Franklin heard. I need you to get it together, sister."

"Half of the office staff here is divorced, single, or using men and women with children for tax purposes," stated Veronica. "At least with Keyshawn, I know he wanted to go all the way in life as lovers. Yes, I got with Keyshawn while he was fooled around earlier on, but the man has changed. He honed in on me. He was only about me!"

"Oh my goodness, girl, he's a thug! Sometimes, love just won't let go, but you have to learn how to wild animals go. You only keep the ones you can control and tame."

"He's not an animal! He's a man! And stop calling him a thug, as if that is so bad anyways."

"You're crazy. Keyshawn's education is probably at tops, from community college, if that." Ms. Cobblestone lifted her chin high. "You saw Police Tales! He hides drugs in his car and does a little drinking and driving. And once a cheater, always a cheater."

"Do you want to know what I think?"

"What?"

Veronica cleared her throat. "I think you like Carl Cleveland."

"Who doesn't, Veronica? He is the *perfect* man."

"Well, I don't want the *perfect* man." Veronica stood tall. "I want a man who is going to take care of me, in a way that God intends. Keyshawn is a saint and doesn't even know it."

"You know that Carl Cleveland is God's gift to women, right?"

"No, he isn't," replied Veronica. "What was I thinking to have listened to any of you in this place? And Ms. Cobblestone, you're the worst of the worst when it comes to advising. It's your fault I dumped the love of my life!"

Ms. Cobblestone sat in her chair. "You look like a queen with Carl Cleveland, but with Keyshawn, you look like a crack whore. Don't get mad because I'm only honest. If you want to stay a sperm bucket for Keyshawn, that's on you. Go on and carry a loser. You cannot work here if you're deciding to go back."

"You're firing me for being with Keyshawn? You cannot do that! I'll complain to Mr. Franklin!"

"Don't waste your time," said Ms. Cobblestone. "One call to

his wife about the affair I've had with him, and he'll lose everything. Therefore, he won't listen to you. I run this place, bitch."

Veronica shook her head as she calculated what she should do next. She did not want to lose her job.

"You cannot decide what to do," said Ms. Cobblestone. "Well, let me tell you what I see. You're going to walk out of this place and run back to that sorry little punk thug of yours. A few minutes later, I will leave this building and find Carl Cleveland."

"Good luck with that!"

"Oh, I have had nothing but luck with Carl. The other day when you were at the set, why do you think the trailer was rocking?"

"What?"

"You stood outside his trailer, waiting for him to shower. I was inside having an orgy with his bodyguards! Then Carl joined with his reconstructed love machine between his legs! I cannot tell you how good it was, but you're a fool to pass up that kind of weapon. Another person's trash is another person's treasure!"

"Wait!" Veronica was shocked. "You had sex with Carl Cleveland, while I was dating him?"

"Every… damn day, bitch." Ms. Cobblestone stood from her chair. She licked her finger and browsed her body down to her crotch with it. "Don't hate the player; try hating the game. Carl makes men like Keyshawn look like they haven't reached puberty!"

"That's not okay!" Veronica got in Ms. Cobblestone's face.

Ms. Cobblestone felt threatened and swung a vicious right at Veronica's face! "Get out of my face, Veronica!"

Slap!

Veronica chuckled. "Oh, no, you didn't! I can call the cops up here right now and have you arrested for assault!"

"Yeah, right," laughed Ms. Cobblestone. "I've slept with judges and high ranking officers. I'd be out in a night in less than half an hour because I'm rich. I am untouchable, and you're just that token Negro around the office! The government forced me to hire one."

Whack!

Veronica slapped the skin off Ms. Cobblestone, who stumbled back against the wall and then forward onto her desk! When Ms. Cobblestone lifted her head, Veronica's entire hand was imprinted across her boss' noggin.

"That was in self-defense, bitch!"

"Get the hell out of here, Veronica!"

"How about we finish what you started outside?"

"Anytime and anyplace, sister, I'm sick of all of your drama!"

"Well, let's go."

"Even better, Veronica, you're fired! You'll never work in this town again! Now get out of my office... You scum!"

"Ooh... You ugly bitch, you're going to get your ass kicked!"

"Get out, Veronica!" shouted Ms. Cobblestone. "I will call security if you don't, you ho! I hate you!"

"Ho? You don't let me catch you out in the street!"

"Oh, you'd better not let me catch you in the street either!"

"Oh yeah, or what're you going to do? Huh? What're you going to do, bitch? What?"

"You're just as bad as Keyshawn, with that gangster talk!" shouted Ms. Cobblestone. She watched Veronica storm out of her office, as co-workers moved out of the way. "You've made the biggest mistake of your life, putting your hands on me, Veronica. When you fall on your face, do not run back to this company!"

Mr. Franklin walked into Ms. Cobblestone's office. "Now, let's just calm down! What a day, eh? Ms. Cobblestone, we sure as hell don't need that kind of employee around here. Let me close this door before I continue. Now, are you okay? Why don't you take a break, maybe go and get some coffee? You look a mess. That young lady slapped the shit out of you; your face is bleeding."

"I should take a break. Thank you, Mr. Franklin."

Mr. Franklin and Ms. Cobblestone left the office and assured their associates that all was well, as they smiled.

"Alright, everyone needs to get back to work!" demanded Mr.

Franklin. He followed Ms. Cobblestone out to the hallway. "You just take some deep breaths, and in a while, we'll go over this project, which is going on on the other side of town. Take a couple of hours until your head is clear. I know that you thought a lot about Veronica. She was one of our best. It's Friday, so usually, there's a great discount on coffee down the block. Go on and get a cup."

"Okay, thanks, Mr. Franklin. I'll be back."

Ms. Cobblestone elegantly walked into the elevator and pushed the button for the parking lot. She took a few more deep breaths and stepped out of the elevator when the bell chimed.

She strolled to her car and pulled keys from her purse.

Whack!

"Oh, I'll show you a thug!" Veronica snatched Ms. Cobblestone by the hair. "You sleep with Carl every day, bitch?"

"I didn't see a ring on his finger!" Ms. Cobblestone screamed. "What difference does it make? You're going back to that gangster thug! And you should because you're just as pitiful as he!"

Ms. Cobblestone got clocked in the back of her head by a fist! Then the old boss bounced off the car door to the ground! Everything in her purse floated in radiator fluid, her earrings rolled away, her saggy breasts and butt flopped from her clothing for the world to see, and her gum sat plastered on her car window.

"What are you doing?" whined Ms. Cobblestone. She was restrained to the ground. "Veronica, you'll never get away with this!"

"It is self-defense, bitch!"

Whud! Whack! Whud! Whud!

After delivering blows to the back of her boss, Veronica angrily yanked an entire side of brunette and grey hair from Ms. Cobblestone's head! *Rip!*

"Ah!" cried Ms. Cobblestone. She had run out of gas, as Veronica had a bunch of hair in her hands. "Let go of my hair, bitch! You are hurting me! Stop, Veronica! I'm going to get you back for this! You can forget about me calling the cops; I'm coming for you when this is all over! You don't know what you've started!"

"You should've never crossed me!"

As the old diva waved for mercy, Veronica threw a wild haymaker at the back of Ms. Cobblestone's head!

Whack! Ms. Cobblestone got knocked the hell out. She laid silent, face down, with her breasts hanging out like an extra set of arms. She looked like a crushed arachnid.

Veronica held up two middle fingers to a loopy Ms. Cobblestone and then ran to the nearest security camera and quickly removed the sock from blocking the lens. Even if investigated, Mr. Franklin made sure to immediately delete the violent footage as payback at Ms. Cobblestone and her constant blackmailing.

"Those who know won't tell and those who tell... Those employees won't have a job." That is what Mr. Franklin told his loyal security team, who finished off a big bag of popcorn they shared during the lynching. Then he declared victory, "Ms. Cobblestone, justice was served on your punk ass!"

By Ashaki Boelter

Chapter 11

The Booty Call

Boggled and confused, Keyshawn sat on the couch in his and Vern's duplex and reminisced about Veronica. Sometimes, love just wouldn't let go. He sought prayer, words to God, without a number.

"Why are you just staring at the television?" asked Vern. It was late, and he strolled into the kitchen for a drink. "Man, all day at work today, you were like a zombie. It's Friday night, and you're sitting there like a ghost! I would say that maybe we should hit the club, but you're a mess. Instead, you should try to get some sleep."

"I know, dude. I just can't sleep. I miss Veronica."

"Keyshawn, what in the hell is wrong with you?"

"Everything is wrong."

"What? The booty ain't good enough with Grand Camorra?"

"There's more than just some booty when it comes to love. It's like, I just can't let go of Veronica. Sometimes, I think I've moved on, but then she just comes back and clouds my mind, body, and soul."

Vern smacked his lips. "Wait a minute. I think I've figured out what you've been saying all along. You can't handle somebody like Grand Camorra! Of course, that's it. Look, bro, I got something to help you with that. Know what I'm saying? All you had to do was ask! In the bathroom cabinet, there are blue pills in the black box next to the condoms."

"I don't feel like talking about it, and it isn't that I can't get it up. I have a headache, Vern. Do you have any aspirins?

"In the bathroom, under the sink, you'll find some Head Numb Aspirin. Just be prepared for drowsiness or sleepiness. I usually sleep until the morning when I take it. Nothing wakes me up! When I finally do get up, though, the headaches are gone."

Keyshawn poured himself a glass of water and went to take a couple of those pills.

Vern looked at some mail on the kitchen table. "I don't know why you're still interested in Veronica. You know Carl is all up in her. You have to face it that she's gone, man. Know what I'm saying? She isn't calling you or seeing you, so move on and give it a rest. You're talking about Veronica Evans and the legendary movie pimp, hooking up. Then you want to fit in that, a regular guy. Just quit."

"You're probably right." Keyshawn returned after taking the pills and crashed on the couch.

"I am right. I'm your boy, aren't I?"

"Yeah, we're boys."

Vern sniffed. "What I want to know is what's so wrong with Grand Camorra? Veronica keeps coming back into your head and shit, but Grand Camorra is even more bodacious! Know what I'm saying?

You've got the perfect woman in your grasp!"

"No one woman is perfect."

"Grand Camorra is!" Vern lifted an eyebrow. "Wait for a second, Key. She doesn't stink down there below the hips, does she? I mean… I've dealt with yeasty, sardine odors before with a simple concoction of baking soda and peroxide, and some aromatherapy candles on the side. I've got all that stuff in the kitchen if that's the case. Know what I'm saying? Vinegar..."

"Vern, I'm going to lay down now. I think the medicine is kicking in because I feel dizzy already. We're both off tomorrow, so maybe we can continue this talk then. Are you going out tonight?"

"No, I'm just going to kick it for tonight and watch a little tube. Know what I'm saying? I think there's a party tomorrow night though. Maybe you'll be up to that and bring Grand Camorra?"

"Good night."

"Good night. Do you need any more sheets or blankets?"

"I'm good."

"Alright, dude, get your rest. I'll see you in the morning."

The midnight hour of the night was blissfully peaceful through the usual melody of first responder sirens, Keyshawn remained in a deep relaxing sleep, and Vern stared at the television from the bed.

"There ain't nothing' on television tonight," whispered Vern. He turned on his red light lamp, climbed from his bed, and wandered to the refrigerator for something to drink. "Damn. I'm almost out of beer. I wonder if Keyshawn got some money in his wallet."

Suddenly, there was a quiet knock at the front door. Startled, Vern dropped Keyshawn's wallet and quickly grabbed a gun from his secret compartment underneath his refrigerator. He tiptoed to the front door. He looked through the peephole.

"Is that Grand Camorra?" he whispered. Vern quickly tiptoed back to the kitchen to stash the gun. On his way back to the front door, he loudly stubbed his toe against the wide cherry end table leg! He internalized his scream but noted that Keyshawn was still completely knocked out from the over-the-counter drug.

The knock at the door repeated. A female whispered, "Keyshawn, are you awake?"

"She's here for a booty call," thought Vern. He looked at his pal on the couch, looked at the door, and looked back at Keyshawn. Vern quickly tiptoed to the kitchen table, grabbed the tablecloth off of it, and flung it over Keyshawn's face! He dashed back to the front door and quietly opened it with his head down.

"I know it's late and all," explained Olivia, "but I need to be with you tonight. I noticed the little bit of light coming from your bedroom window, so I figured you might still be up. By the way, why don't you keep the porch light on at night? That way, people could see if someone was trying to break into your house."

"Uh-huh, come in," mumbled Vern. He tried to imitate Keyshawn's voice and softly coughed.

It was so dark in the duplex; he grabbed her arm and led her through the living room where Keyshawn slept.

"Why don't you turn a light on?" she whispered.

"My roommate would see it through the cracks of his door and wake up." Vern maneuvered her down the hall, towards his bedroom. "We don't want to wake my homeboy at this hour; he can be an ass when he's half asleep. Now, come on."

"Was there someone on the couch back there?" asked Olivia.

"That's just some laundry and probably my roommate's snoring cat that loves to sleep in it."

"Your voice sounds terrible. You sound sick."

"It's just an allergic reaction to the cat," whispered Vern. "Know what I'm saying? Now, just follow me. Okay, wait here. Do not move. I'll be right back."

Before Vern led her into his bedroom, he turned off the red lights and the television. Now the room was black. "Okay, come inside."

"Why does it have to be so dark in here?"

"It is kind of messy in here with moving boxes and all." Vern continued the lies. "I just moved in recently. Now keep it down. My

136

homeboy is in the other room across the hall."

The door across the hall was the door to the bathroom. There was only one bedroom in the place.

"Do you want me, Keyshawn? Do you want my body?"

"Hell yeah, I want your body," Vern whispered. He dropped his clothing. He reached for her throughout the darkness. "Dang girl, where'd you go?"

"You really should consider taking a cough drop for your throat, at least. You sound so different. It isn't contagious, is it?"

"An allergy is not contagious! Know what I'm saying? Now, bring that big old booty over here, Grand Camorra! Ugh!"

"You don't have to call me Grand Camorra, you know. I'm not acting right now. Please call me, Olivia."

"Whatever." He savagely removed her clothing, positioned her on her knees, and he smacked the hell out of her buttocks.

"Oh my goodness, you know what you like!" Olivia slightly felt pain but was suddenly overwhelmed with bike-pumping gusts that dented her expanded heart. She was utterly in love, no matter the swelling and head injuries she sustained with bumping the wooden headboard. "That's what I like! Oh, yes!"

"Olivia!" Vern huffed. "You need to fix your wig. It's sliding off to the right. Gal, keep it coming!"

"You got it, daddy!"

"Be quiet and don't wake up my homie; I'm almost done!" Vern stuffed the end of his pillow into her big mouth! He knew Keyshawn would surely kill him if he knew what was going on in that bedroom. Olivia mumbled louder through the sheets and cushions, as Vern had a handful of her hair and directed her like a horse on how to turn her moistened, cocoa hips.

Three minutes passed. Vern had done his thing and fought not to fall asleep. He was proud of his damage tonight and hoped that it was enough for her to turn up her relationship with his homie. That way, Keyshawn would never turn his thoughts away from Olivia. In other words, he did not have to listen to or see any more sobbing over

Veronica. He calmly asked, "So, did I lock this up? Huh? You're my gal now, right? Say something!"

"Keyshawn, I'm yours forever!"

"Perfect. I can see that my job is done here. Now beat it." Vern got up and twistedly figured that he locked in Keyshawn and Olivia for good. Olivia would never let Keyshawn walk away or get away with talking about Veronica now! "I'll walk you to the door."

"What?"

"What do you mean *what*?"

"Why can't I sleep here? Just let me sleep with you until the morning. I'm too tired to drive back to where I'm staying. I'm staying across town, and it's dangerous out here at this time of night. I saw somebody get robbed a few blocks away from here!"

Vern grabbed her belongings and said, "We can't sleep together here because my homie and I agreed not to have women sleepover. It's just part of the rules we have. If we didn't have that rule, my attractive roommate, Vern, would have several women over every night. He's unbelievable with women!"

"He sounds like he's good with men too, I mean for giving you a place to stay after leaving Veronica, of course."

"He's a damn great guy! Now Olivia, let me get the door."

"Before I go, can I kiss you for the road?"

Vern placed his palm to her face, while in the darkness. He knew that she would figure he wasn't Keyshawn if he kissed her.

"Keyshawn, you're not going to kiss me?"

"Baby, you're a little messy right now, around the mouth, from all the stuff we did. Know what I'm saying? Maybe, we should save that kiss for tomorrow. And fix your wig." He softly coughed.

"I think I love you! You're the greatest, Keyshawn. As long as you don't get sicker, we're still on for a late lunch, right?"

"No doubt," answered Vern. He wanted to be there instead of Keyshawn, after the sex he just experienced with Olivia. That would take a miracle, being that she was not his. Nope. His old pal, still out cold from the over-the-counter medication and hidden under the laundry on the couch, had Olivia by the heart.

"I'm never leaving you," whispered Olivia.

"Bye. Drive safely." Vern quietly closed the front door after he watched Olivia make it to her car. He thought to himself, "What a dream-come-true! I got a piece of Grand Camorra's big old ass!"

Olivia drove away like a drunken driver, but she hadn't gone far. She pulled over in front of the neighbor's home and fell asleep until the sun came up because she was worn out.

The very next morning, Keyshawn woke up to a very delicious smell. Someone was in the kitchen and cooked seasoned eggs, grits, buttermilk biscuits, and sugared maple sausages. He rolled off of the couch, walked into the kitchen, and found Olivia preparing breakfast!

"Olivia, what are you doing here?"

"Good morning, sunshine!" she greeted. "Well, at least you sound okay this morning. I was worried you might have come down with something serious. Did you sleep on the couch?"

Keyshawn nodded. "I think the headache is subsiding."

Olivia smiled because she figured that she wore him out so badly last night; he could not make it back to the bedroom. "At least your head feels better, Keyshawn. My head feels like it was attacked by woodpeckers, but I'll be okay. Go on and have a seat. Have I told you that you're the man?"

"Thanks?"

Olivia kissed Keyshawn on his forehead. "I love you."

"Is my roommate still around? How did you get in the house?"

"No," answered Olivia. "When I called you on my cellular phone about thirty minutes ago to check on you this morning, he answered and said you were probably going to wake up soon. Vern had errands to run but said the house is good as ours, and maybe I could cook something to put a little pep into your step. Was he a little sick too? He didn't sound as well, either. Anyways, he left the front door unlocked for me."

Keyshawn studied Olivia's lovely legs up to her mid-thighs. She probably displayed that much leg on purpose from the looks of what she wore. However, he kind of grew sour when he noticed a few black finger marks on her calf and thigh.

"I miss the simple life," stated Olivia. "I haven't cooked for a man who I love, in many years. And I sure do miss the smell of neighborhoods like this. It smells so real."

"What does that mean, Olivia? You said it smells *so real*."

"It smells like a genuine ghetto."

Keyshawn didn't particularly care for that statement. "This isn't a ghetto. It is considered a middle-class neighborhood with some misfortunate families here and there."

"I looked out the window and only saw mostly black people," explained Olivia. "There are broken-down cars all over the place. There is graffiti spray-painted on a lot of property! Those are signs of gangs and danger, so I would say yes, this is the ghetto."

Keyshawn was irritably perturbed, but the current conversation wasn't the only source of that. "Olivia, I've watched the news and read a lot of articles about school shootings and meth or drugs taking over predominantly white neighborhoods. No doubt, those are signs of danger, but nobody calls those ghettos."

"Gee Keyshawn, maybe I should leave? What in the hell has gotten into you this morning? Why are you acting like that?"

Keyshawn had to get something off of his chest. "So, what was up with the sex scene you put on at the studios in front of me? I know you fucked that dude on the set!

"Is that what this snotty attitude is about? Damn Keyshawn, I cannot imagine how you'd react with me doing a love scene with a woman. Yep, I do that from time to time too! Do you have a problem with that?"

"Oh, hell, to the no, I won't accept behavior with a woman I date! I don't care if it's acting or not! I don't want a woman sharing her lips and all with anybody else!"

"Well, maybe we should've talked about all this last night!"

"I was too tired to talk last night!"

"I bet you were!" Olivia was raged as she felt disrespected and used. She could not understand how Keyshawn was so closed-minded in these times; just about everyone in society gave up being old-fashioned. She pulled off her wig and shouted, "This morning, you're an ass, sucker! You're lucky I'm willing to fix this because I'm in love with you!"

"Whoa! You wear a wig?"

"What do you mean by that?" Olivia was confused because last night, she was told to straighten it during the sexual rendezvous.

However, Keyshawn thought his comment was insensitive. What if she wore a wig for a medical reason?

"Olivia, I'm sorry. I think that I need some space this morning. I appreciate you making me breakfast, but I would appreciate it if you left for a little bit."

Olivia placed a hand on Keyshawn's forehead. "Yeah, you're a little warm. I'll put the food away and let you rest. Just remember that I'm yours, and I'm never letting you go. And while I'm away, promise me that you'll get rid of that stinky attitude. We'll talk about the acting stuff I do too. And don't forget to turn the oven off; I'll see you at lunch. Bye."

Keyshawn did not understand her newly clinginess and watched her finally drive away in her limousine that no longer had hubcaps and windows on it. He thought most women would've never wanted to return after an argument like that! She was gone for now.

What was also absent was his desire of Olivia, ever since watching her make out the other day on the set. A few years back, he may have wanted a girlfriend like her, but today he wanted a stable relationship of his own. He did not want his woman to share kisses with another person, acting or not. He did not need eye candy, as he knew a lot of men would stare her down in front of him; he was a jealous dude. Perhaps Olivia was his just a rebound, but this morning he wanted a long shot, game-winner.

Keyshawn sat back at the kitchen table. He'd run out of good friends that could help him make the right decision about staying with or leaving Olivia. Everybody in the world that knew of the relationship pushed Keyshawn to date her! She was famous and beautiful, but Keyshawn's heart was with Veronica. He wouldn't count on anyone's advice, especially to avoid looking like a fool.

"Lord, help me." He knew Olivia was coming back around lunchtime. So, after he called on his heavenly father, he picked up his cell phone and called his earthly dad.

"Son, how are you doing?" Keyshawn's father was excited! "When I'd heard that you lost Veronica, I thought you'd never bounce back. But I prayed, and it was the Lord that delivered you from Veronica Evans to Grand Camorra! That is a miracle, which I hope, you can testify about when you show up to the church. And between you and me, son, Grand Camorra is the hottest woman on the planet! Do not repeat that to your mother."

"Dad, I like her, but she's too much."

"What? The Lord will never give us more than we can handle, and you won't find anyone hotter than her."

"I'm still in love with Veronica, dad. We used to have so much fun going on picnics, balling, and just being real."

"It's Grand Camorra, son! You're young, so live it up until you want to lock something down."

"I don't know that I trust her as I should."

"What is bothering you, son?"

"I don't like sharing my girl with other dudes or women, whether she's acting or not. The other day, I watched her on a movie,

142

doing a love scene, and I was turned off."

"Do you know how crazy you sound? You watched her making out in a movie, and you were turned off? Have you talked to her about how you feel, son?"

Suddenly, Keyshawn's mother picked up the other house phone. "Hello, Keyshawn, its mom. I've been listening to your father, and it sounds like you have a problem dating Grand Camorra?"

His dad answered, "Honey, our son says that he can't trust her basically because she's too sexy for him. I don't think Keyshawn knows what to do with that. And he's still got something for Veronica Evans, the one who dumped him for Carl Cleveland, a joker who is about our age!"

"Are you for real, Keyshawn?" His mother rolled her eyes. "Veronica dumped you like a bag of trash! Quit thinking about that skinny heifer and look at what the Lord has given you now, son!"

"I cannot handle being with Grand Camorra."

Keyshawn's mother was instantly livid. "You couldn't handle Veronica Evans either. Who can you handle? Keyshawn, I didn't raise a fool! Your father and I would love to meet Grand Camorra before you cut her out. I'm sure that we could iron some things out. She seems like a reasonable person when I see her doing the weather on television and like a very nice young woman."

"Grand Camorra is the ticket!" Keyshawn's father was set on the local star. "You *can* handle Grand Camorra!"

"That's right," said his mother.

"I don't condone sex before marriage," said his father, "but you can straighten out the trust issues with her in the bedroom; it only takes one time! There doesn't have to be a conversation about it. Show Grand Camorra, who is boss, son! She'll come around. You're a Jackson, so I know that you got the necessary tools, son!"

"Honey!" screamed Keyshawn's mother. She was ashamed and giggled. "You do know that I'm on the line, right? For heaven's sake, this is your son that you're talking to!"

Keyshawn listened to his mother and father quarrel over the phone about changing Grand Camorra to his liking.

"Mom and dad, I think I'd better go now."

"Son," said Keyshawn's mother, "I'm sorry that we don't have the answers you need. We're not perfect; nobody's perfect. The best advice I'll give you is to go to God with your troubles."

"That's right, son!" shouted Keyshawn's father. "Your mom is one-hundred percent right. You should give it to God. As a matter of fact, why don't you come to church tomorrow? Bring Grand Camorra with you. Let the Lord do his miraculous work on the both of you."

"Your father is right."

"Mom, I haven't been to church in a while."

Keyshawn's father replied, "Do you even know if she even believes in God?"

"I don't know."

"You were raised in the church," added his mother. "How do you date somebody and not know what they believe, if at all?"

"Honey," his dad interrupted, "perhaps Keyshawn got with her for one thing. After all, she is Grand Camorra! Maybe it just turned into a relationship."

Keyshawn answered his father, "I was looking for a relationship with her. I wasn't thinking about Christianity at the time."

"Well, with the recent garbage you've dealt with, maybe you should." His mother was agitated. "You've been out there in the streets too much, hanging with that silly thug. You need to return to the church and repent. Allow the Lord to reveal what you should do next! Now, I would like it if you bring her to church tomorrow. We'll plan to eat out afterword. I believe that the Lord can do something for you two. Come to church, son."

"How did his dilemma become about going to church?" Keyshawn thought, but he agreed to go just to give it a rest, already. After all, church service was only two hours out of 24 hours in a day.

"Okay," Keyshawn obliged. He planned to cancel the lunch today with a phone call, so that's when he planned to invite her to church tomorrow. "I'll be there. I'll check with her. I don't see her coming, though; she doesn't come off churchy."

144

"Let go and let God!" declared his mother.

Meanwhile, across town in her beautiful home, Veronica Evans sat on a stool across from the couch Carl Cleveland slid his nasty buttocks off of, and talked to her parents, Ed and Cindy Evans, on the cell phone.

"We've taken yoga classes, gone to expensive restaurants, and had a few laughs about various celebrity gossips," said Veronica. Even though she had her couch professionally cleaned of his leaked boo-boo, she still could see the unmatched curved and shaded microfiber. "He is an interesting man, full of surprises. Unfortunately, mom, I'm just not as into him as I would like to be."

Veronica's mother loved Carl Cleveland; she'd been a fan of his romance movies for some time. She was a little stunned by her daughter's admission of dislike in him. "He came from New York to be closer to you; at least, that's what I read in the magazine article I recently read recently."

"Sure, he has dropped me off and picked me up from work nearly every day while he's here. However, he is going to return to New York in a few weeks."

"Veronica, you know that comes with the business. You're an astonishing celebrity as well. You're so well-known that you could easily find work out east, should you settle with. So, why do you feel like you're not into him? Was it something he said or did?"

Veronica's nose flared as she imaged a whiff of the couch where Carl vacated some dookie butter that penetrated her soul. Her toes curled, his shoulders lifted high, and a shiver came upon her.

"I don't know," continued Ed, "he sounds like a good man from the articles I've read. I don't ever watch his movies you're your mother does, but I'd love to meet the fellow. Perhaps we can help you discover what you want. The last guy you had, we told you ahead of time how that was going to turn out. You have to leave those thugs alone. That is certainly a step up in the right direction."

Cindy said, "I heard that you left your job. I guess we, along with half of America perhaps, thought you might be moving in with Carl and preparing to wed. Why would you have to work, living with him? He's loaded!"

"Sign the prenuptial!" shouted her father.

Veronica chuckled. "No, I left She's Golden to start my new job at City Beat Magazine on Monday. I figured it best to leave because we did not share the same values at the end of the day."

Veronica's mother heard her but daydreamed of her daughter with diamonds draped around her neck on a remote island with Carl-cloned babies dancing around her. "You shouldn't have to work another day in your life if you can play the cards right with Carl!"

"I don't think he's the best fit."

"What do you mean he's not the best fit?"

Mr. Evans added, "He is kind of old, honey."

Cindy snatched the cell phone from her husband, turned off the speakerphone function, and placed the cell phone to her ear. "Don't listen to your father; he's aged horribly. Trust me. So Veronica, what do you mean you don't think he's the best fit? Is he, blue pill dependent or something?"

"Ewe, mom, I wasn't literal." Veronica clarified. "I meant that I don't think we are a good match."

"But he's sexy as hell, and he's filthy rich, unlike that joke you were sleeping under! What was that thug's name again?"

"His name is Keyshawn."

"I'm glad that you got up from underneath that bum," replied her mother. "He worked from a dirty warehouse, over sixty hours a week on minimum wage, and the one time I met him, he was sagging his pants and walked like a penguin. With his hat on backward, he couldn't even talk in clear English, using all that slang filth. That's not a real man. You've done a 180 from that bum by dating Carl Cleveland, who dresses nice and is articulate. He's a great actor!"

"He's a great success!" Veronica's dad added. He stood behind Veronica's mother. "Carl is the image of the perfect black man in movies, from action to romance. He's a keeper!"

Cindy interrupted, "He warms me up for your father!"

Ed wasn't surprised, nor was he ashamed because he had guilt for leaving the television on when they had sex. He had the news on every time, waiting for the sexy meteorologist, Grand Camorra, to get him over the hump with Cindy. He kept his mouth shut.

"That's all that the media shows you of him," replied Veronica. "You don't know the man. Sure, he's a great actor, but he's terrible in person. I don't trust him anymore, and I am going to dump him."

"You don't trust him? What did he do?"

Veronica's dad quickly snatched the phone. "Veronica? Honey, what in the living hell is wrong with you? Carl Cleveland is as sharp as a man could be! He's exactly the kind of man *you need*."

"How are you going to tell me what I need, dad?"

"I'm your father! That's how! Now, you bring that movie star home so we can meet him. Your mother and I can relate to him and help fix the problem. He's a little older, but I can sleep at night knowing you're with him instead of with that nut job you were with."

"I think I'm still in love with Keyshawn," whispered Veronica. "We've built many fond memories already. I cannot help to think that sometimes, love just won't let go."

"Cindy, our daughter has lost her mind!"

Veronica shouted, "Dad!"

Mrs. Evans spoke. "Now, let us be reasonable. We all know that Carl Cleveland is a mature man, who is successful with money. From what we've learned of Keyshawn, he's a hoodlum. Veronica, we raised you to do nothing but succeed in everything you do. Keyshawn has not succeeded in anything that I recall."

"I sure as hell don't know of anything he's succeeded in," added her husband.

Veronica took no offense. Everybody she knew had the same opinion of Keyshawn. So she tried to share some memorable moments with her parents that she favored. "I remember a time when we were planning to go to a gangster rap concert, but before we went, he took me to the chicken place downtown. He accidently dropped his barbeque chicken on his crotch and he sold those tickets to buy me a beautiful fur coat. He cares about me."

"He's a thug, honey," said her dad.

"Also, there was a time when we went bowling, and he slipped and fell on his butt! I had to call an ambulance, and he ended up having to get stitches on the back of his head. We laughed for days about that! And he really appreciated me being there for him."

"What?" Veronica's father roared into the receiver. "You're still into Keyshawn? I'm done! Here's your mother. I can't talk to you right now. I can't even think! You've got Carl Cleveland in your hands, and you want to throw him away for some trash! I'm going to the golf course to clear my head!"

"I can't help it, dad," said Veronica. "Nobody has ever understood me the way Keyshawn does. And nobody's perfect."

Veronica's father, Ed, gave the phone to his wife, paced, and swore in the background. He absentmindedly looked for his clubs.

"Veronica, now you listen," said her mother, calmed and all. "It's time to grow up now. I want you to stop being this little girl trying to get back at your parents by dating a gangster thug. Sure, we were overprotecting of you when you were younger, but—."

Veronica's father snatched the phone back from her mother! He shouted at his daughter, "I swear that if you ever bring that Keyshawn around here, I will call the freaking cops! I swear it!"

"Honey," said his wife, "you need to take a deep breath and then reason with her. You're going to give yourself a stroke, just like your sister Bertha's husband, if you don't calm down!"

By Ashaki Boelter

"Do what? Are you out of your mind?" Ed Evans sprayed and slobbered all over the phone receiver. "I don't need to calm down! Veronica, don't you dare come home for Christmas! We should've never adopted this girl, Cindy!"

Click! Veronica's father hung up on his daughter!

"Hello? Hello?" Veronica couldn't believe it. "Hello? Oh, my god. Are you kidding me? Why is it that everybody has a fantasy about who I should be with and won't respect or address what I feel my needs are? It is my life, not anybody else's, and I only get one shot at it."

By Ashaki Boelter

Chapter 12

The Truth Shall Set You Free

"Let the church say, '*Amen*'!"

The New Birth Baptist Church erupted from the foundation, as the pastor preached a fiery sermon that brought half the church to the altar for God's forgiveness, to be saved, healed, and prayed for. The pastor threw it out from his studies of the Bible that everybody was short of His glory, but only God judged. And if anybody died today, would they have honestly believed that they were a shoo-in for the kingdom of God? The pastor wanted his saints to be set free from any bondage, any sin, and any tribulation.

"Somebody else is out there struggling!" bellowed the pastor. "Somebody needs the Lord! We're still waiting, as the Lord is telling me that there is still someone out there that needs to confess and come

151

clean! I know the service is going long, but don't resist the Lord tugging at your heart. You know who you are, so get up from that pew and come on down! The alter waits. Gone and give it to Jesus Christ, who died on the cross for your sins! Let Him set you free!"

"He is so good," whispered Olivia, who sat next to Keyshawn in a pew with his mother and father. She decided to come to church since she sensed something was wrong with her man yesterday, probable guilt from the late Friday night booty call. He did not want to do lunch Saturday, so she hadn't seen him since yesterday morning. Because of the middle of the night, Friday, Olivia was blindly hooked.

Keyshawn's mother overheard and grinned with success.

"He's been preaching like that forever," stated Keyshawn. "He isn't slowing down either. I've been going here since I was a kid."

"Oh-oh, the pastor is looking directly at me." Olivia ducked.

"No, he can't be."

"Yes, he is, Keyshawn. Look."

The pastor shouted, "Tell the truth!"

Keyshawn looked back and forth. "Oh my goodness, Olivia, he is looking at you! Maybe you need to go on down to the altar? It can't hurt anything. Just go down there and close your eyes! Whatever happens... happens."

"Oh, uh-uh, I don't think so."

Keyshawn's mother hunched over and spoke at Olivia. "All the flirting that you do on the news and the slutty roles you played on soaps and television movies, maybe you should think about purifying some of your life. It's good for the soul. Have you ever accepted Jesus Christ as your savior?"

Olivia replied, "I'm a Christian. It's just that anything we celebrities do, it becomes overblown, and it could ruin my reputation. My agent always warns me to be careful, and since she's not here, I have to watch myself in the public eye. I don't want to offend the people that put money in my pockets, who may not agree with seeing me here. Remember, I have agents and production people and bodyguards who are employed under me too. I cannot lose profits."

"Darling," Keyshawn's mother replied, "you're offending God by talking like that. Would you put your career ahead of everlasting life in Heaven? It was the Lord that got you this far. Now, you go on down to the altar and at least give thanks to the Lord."

"You're right." Olivia respected motherly advice.

Keyshawn offered to walk her down the aisle. Mostly to let the brothers of the church know that she was with him. He nodded, fist-bumped, and high fived some of his old friends on the way down.

"Well, praise His name!" shouted the pastor. He hopped like a bunny rabbit in place with the microphone in one hand and held his hand up in the air. As his belly-flopped around in his robe, he shook his head left to right and puckered his lips as if something was sour. "Jesus! Jesus! Jesus! Glory to God! We have Grand Camorra down at the altar! Whoa, the Lord is good! Let the church say, Halleluiah!"

"Yes!" Keyshawn celebrated, as he watched his mother rejoice from the pew. She bounced around and cried while she shouted tongues and waved her bulletin as a fan to cool herself off.

"Can I get a few more brothers and sisters down here to lay hands on these folks?" asked the pastor.

Keyshawn closed his eyes, for he hadn't prayed for quite some time. It wasn't hard to do, though.

The entire church nearly filled the altar, as a lot of youth rushed down to get close or touch the popular and beautiful actress.

The worn pastor handed the microphone to his Assistant Pastor to lead the worship. All eyes were closed. The pastor led Grand Camorra from the altar and through the doors to the left. Neither Keyshawn nor the patrons saw the pastor and Grand Camorra exit.

"Come on in," welcomed the pastor. He opened his office door and followed Grand Camorra into his office. "What a service."

"It sure is awesome."

"Have a seat, please, Grand Camorra."

Olivia graciously sat down in the chair across the desk from the pastor. She was sure that he was either going to ask for a donation or maybe about marrying Keyshawn, as she believed most pastors did not agree with sleeping around before marriage. However, the pastor sat and just gave her a particularly angry look.

"Is Grand Camorra your real name?"

"Call me Olivia, pastor."

"Great Olivia," greeted the pastor. He turned around and poured himself a glass of water. Then he returned to face his client and placed his cell phone on the desk. "Is Olivia your real name?"

"What do you mean? Of course, it is."

"You can't keep lying," said the pastor. "Please, don't you sit there and act like you don't know what I'm talking about. I am a man of God, and this is the Lord's house. We try to keep the lies out of the church, even though sometimes that doesn't happen."

Olivia suddenly felt attacked. She chuckled. "Why did you bring me down here to this dungeon? You do have a service to finish up. I dug what you preached, but this is weird."

"That boy, Keyshawn, you're seeing; his parents told me you'd be here. I did a little research on you."

"Okay… So, you want an autograph?"

"Cut out the games with me. Keyshawn doesn't know, does

154

he? I don't appreciate you being involved with a family I sincerely appreciate, without telling the truth about who you are."

"What I have with my man is none of your business," stated Olivia. "Now, I don't know what you think you know, but this meeting is over! Thank you and goodbye, pastor."

"You walk out of this office like that, and I promise you that your career will be in jeopardy! You stand there until I'm done!"

"What is your problem?"

"Now, I'm not going to let you destroy any of the saints in my church. Do you understand me? You're not getting away with this, not this time!"

"I came to church to accept Jesus Christ. It's between you and God, whatever you think you got on me. You have no right to condemn me. Like you said, only God can judge me."

"How long have you *lied* to that young man?"

"I have not lied to Keyshawn?"

"Don't mess with me." The pastor stood face to face with Olivia. Then he broke out and asked, "How long is it going to be before you tell him that you're *a man*?"

"Oh my goodness, how'd you know?"

"Your real name is Oliver Chris Williams. I did extensive research on you because Keyshawn and his family play an important role in this church family. We have each other's back."

"Well, I'm not a man anymore. That's that. It's not about what you believe to know; it's about my way of thinking. I know who I am. I am a woman. The rest of my business is none of yours."

"Keyshawn doesn't know who you are, so do you not believe that you're dishonest with him? What happens if he finds out that you're a man, and he wanted a woman?"

"First off," explained Oliver, "I am having a sex change operation at the end of the year. I have breast implants. Secondly, we had sex the other night, and he enjoyed me. It's on him that he didn't want more than some booty action. Had he reached around, he would have found out, but I'm sure that it would've been okay because my man was totally into what he found."

The pastor shook his head. "You're deceiving him, and knowing him as the young man I know, I think that you may want to run as far from here as possible before he finds out. I don't think he'll take kindly to how you've deceived him or his family. Straight, gay, or whatever the preference aside, I don't think any person would appreciate this magnitude of being lied to."

"Well, what he doesn't know can't hurt him. So, you keep your mouth shut and preach as your job calls you to do."

"I cannot believe this."

"Look, pastor, I'm not trying to be rude," said Olivia, "but I don't need you lecturing me on how I do my relationship affairs. Who do you think you are? Now, I suppose that you're going to tell me how I'm going to hell for changing my sex?"

"You're right in that I cannot judge you, but God will. All this has very little to do with me and everything with you telling him the truth. The truth will set you free. So, don't go pointing fingers at me or the church for pleading that you tell the truth to another person."

"After my operation, I won't have to worry about a lie."

"You need to tell that man out there the truth!"

"Whatever! We're just going around in circles."

The pastor was very angry and could still hear the worship music. The altar call was still going. "Do you know if Keyshawn wants children of his own?"

"We just started dating, so we're not discussing that!"

"So, you'll wait for a year or so from now?"

"By that time, I will tell him that I can't have kids, or we'll simply adopt a snotty-nosed brat like any other couple."

"You need to be honest, Oliver. NO relationship works with half-truths or dishonesty. Now, as a close friend of Keyshawn's family, I will not allow you to hurt them. I have to share this with them if you don't. I'm not going to harbor such a secret!"

"You had better keep it a secret! And you do not have the right to tell me what I have to do or who I am!"

"You have every right in the world to be gay and dress like a woman because that's your business. I don't hold any hate against you or your choice, but deceiving those close to me, forget me holding that mess in. That's what I'm against, as their friend. I hope that I'm clear about all of that. Are you afraid that Keyshawn will leave your side if he finds out?"

"Listen carefully, holy man." Oliver slid his hand into his purse. "I spent lots of money on this upcoming sex change. I already paid a grip for throat operation and these magnificent boobs. So, you're not going to say a damn thing to Keyshawn. Are we clear?"

"What will you do if I tell?"

"I've got options," replied Oliver. "One option is that I know people; I'm Grand Camorra, the hottest commodity on television! I know underground fighters, mobsters, and arsonists. I could make your life a living hell, if you want to mess with mines, with the snap of a finger. Am I clear, pastor?"

"Is that a threat?"

"Perhaps we can start over," said Oliver. He could not hear noises in the church any longer. Perhaps the church was near dismissal. "How about if I write you a hefty check to keep your mouth shut. I'm sure that there's a nice Cadi you'd like to flaunt or a small jet you could use to expand your ministry. I'll give you a nice amount."

The pastor watched Oliver write a check for $500,000. There in front of him was a paper that would fix every repair and more!

"Goodbye, pastor. That was a great service, by the way."

"That doesn't cut it." The pastor watched Oliver turn away and walk back towards the door that led to the altar. "Get back in here! Are you trying to buy a liar out of me? Keyshawn is my godson, and you've got it twisted!"

"Then, we still have a problem," said Oliver. He tried to pull a small gun from his purse!

The pastor had not moved that fast in decades, but he hurdled over his desk, let his weight control his momentum and he tackled Oliver to the floor to fight for his life!

157

Within sixty seconds, ushers rushed into the pastor's office and stood at the doorway in shock! Other saints heard the noisy scuffle and were shoved away from the office by the shocked ushers!

The pastor and Oliver exchanged punches and grappled all over the office floor, as they broke chairs and knocked pictures from the walls.

"What in the world is going on in there?" Keyshawn got ushered through the crowd and stood inside the doorway with his parents. The ushers closed the door behind them to shield the rest of the church away from the finding. "I cannot believe this! The pastor is trying to get some from my gal?"

The pastor dismounted and stood by Keyshawn's father. "It's not what you think. I swear that there's something you need to know!"

Keyshawn's father stood to the pastor's face. "Man, you've got some serious explaining to do! Can you explain to me what the hell is going on here with you riding my son's girlfriend?"

"Olivia, or whatever you want to be called, would you please tell him the truth now?" asked the pastor.

Olivia flipped her hair from her face and shook her head no.

Keyshawn's dad popped his knuckles. "You've got five seconds to explain to us what is going on. We go back a lot of years. I've come to you about everything in my life, and you're my son's godfather! What are you doing down here with my son's gal with your clothes all hanging out, jack?"

"That is not a woman!" The pastor screamed at the top of his lungs. He wasn't about to get beat up over Oliver's deception.

"You mean Grand Camorra is a man?"

"Yes." The pastor stepped back.

Keyshawn's father calmly turned to his son. "You don't have to lie or pretend, but it is okay. Your mother and I will love you just the same. Go on and be honest with us. Son, are you gay?"

"What the hell is going on around here?" Keyshawn stared at Olivia. "I am not gay. What is everybody talking about? Pastor, what's up with all this about Olivia being a dude! We all just saw you trying to doggy-style my girlfriend! Man, I ought to knock you out!"

Keyshawn's mother stepped in front of her husband and son. "I need everyone to cool down. If Olivia is a man, this mess has to be scary about now. None of this leaves the walls of this church. It's just us here. Without any harm to anybody in the house of the Lord, Olivia, were you born a male or female?"

The rest of the church congregation stood in the lobby with no idea that the Jacksons awaited Grand Camorra's truth about being a male or female. After that, Grand Camorra could simply go on with her celebrity status.

By Ashaki Boelter

Chapter 13

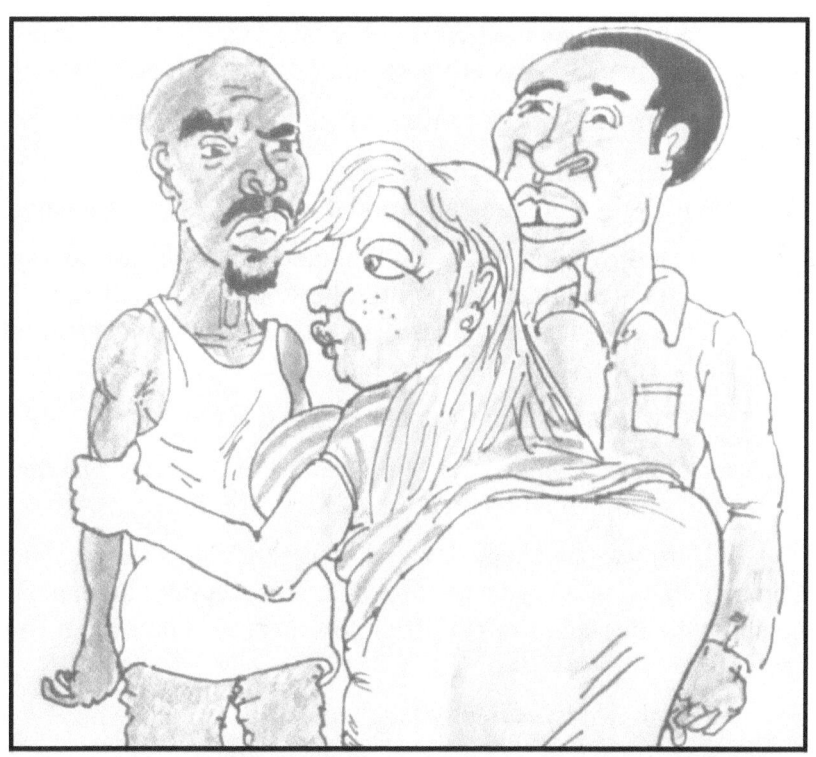

Do You Know What I'm Saying?

"**W**hat's wrong with you? Why'd you slam my front door like that?"

"I just want to take a long, boiling-hot shower."

Vern tried to slow Keyshawn down in the hallway of his apartment. "Chill out, homeboy. It's Vern, man. What happened? You're not supposed to come home from church like this. Know what I'm saying? Calm down!"

Keyshawn stepped around Vern and entered the restroom. He slammed the bathroom door and locked it.

"Hey! Stop slamming all my fucking doors!" shouted Vern. "You need to cool down. Know what I'm saying? Keyshawn!"

Bam! Bam! Bam!

Somebody banged away on the front door.

"What in the blue hell is going on around here?" Vern walked down the hallway to answer the front door. He shouted, "Who is it?"

"Vern, can I speak to Keyshawn, please?"

"Grand Camorra, what is going on?" Vern opened the front door. "Why's my homeboy all worked up like that? What happened?"

"Just move out of my way!" Grand Camorra shoved Vern to the side and entered the apartment. She stood in the hallway. "Keyshawn, I need to talk to you. I need to talk to you because I love you. I'm sorry! Please talk to me!"

"Keyshawn, the gal wants to talk! Get out here!"

Keyshawn walked out of the bathroom. "I want that person out of this place now! Get the hell out of here, you!"

Vern was shocked. "Whoa! Why are you talking to Grand Camorra like that? If you're going to disrespect her like that, then I'd be happy to take this woman off of your hands! Know what I'm saying?"

Keyshawn hysterically laughed. "You can have her!"

The Hollywood star smacked. "Keyshawn, I seem to recall that a couple of nights ago, I had you in ecstasy when we made love in your bedroom. You were thrilled, and I'm sure of that! I could barely walk to the car that night, and I for sure as hell couldn't drive far! It was the best sex I have ever had in my entire life! Don't do this!"

"What in the hell are you talking about?" asked Keyshawn. He opened the door. "We've never done it!"

"Oh? Well, that's a lie!" screamed Grand Camorra. "You took me into your room, shoved a pillow in my mouth, and bashed me into your bedpost for a couple of minutes!"

"Look. I don't know what the hell you're talking about, but I want you to get the hell out of this place!" Keyshawn returned to the bathroom and locked the door.

"Why are you going into Vern's room?" asked Grand Camorra. She looked at Vern. Then she pounded on that bathroom door.

Bam! Bam! Bam!

"Get away from me!" shouted Keyshawn.

"Open this door!" shouted Grand Camorra. "Face up to it that you loved every inch of this body as a man should!"

That had done it. Keyshawn flung open the bathroom door. "You have five seconds to get the hell out of here, or else I'll call the police! I swear that if I ever see you again…"

Keyshawn stepped out of the bathroom, as Grand Camorra noticed the toilet and tub inside.

"That is a bathroom!" Grand Camorra interrupted him.

"Duh," replied Keyshawn.

"You told me Friday night that it was your roommate's room."

Keyshawn was seriously confused now. "I never saw you on Friday night. I was sick Friday night, and after taking pills, I was out for the night."

"You lie! How could you be so rude?"

"I have no idea what you're talking about!"

"You humped my brains out Friday night!"

"We haven't done anything ever!" shouted Keyshawn. "I know that because I'm still in love with Veronica! Friday night, I was out cold on the couch in the living room."

Even Grand Camorra read his honesty. However, she was now confused. "Well, isn't that your room over there?"

Keyshawn figured it out. "Vern, get your ass back here!"

Vern strolled up to the bathroom door with his eyebrows raised and a thumb in his mouth. "I'm sorry, man. You were asleep and well… That's Grand Camorra, man! Know what I'm saying? I couldn't help myself. Know what I'm saying? I'm sorry."

"I'm glad to see the kind of friend you are finally," said Keyshawn. "You slept with my-then interest! That was low, dude!"

"It was dark, and I thought she was my ex-girlfriend."

"Yeah, okay, Vern."

"I was drunk that night, I swear!"

"Quit lying, Vern!" Keyshawn shook his head. "I chugged the last beer after you went to bed. Those headache pills were nasty, so I washed it down. You know, Veronica may have been right about you all along. You're a bad friend with bad advice. So, I always wondered if your wrongdoing would ever come back to bite you. And I think it has! Congratulations, Grand Camorra, is yours."

"Pal, this is the kindest thing you've ever done for me." Vern placed his arm around the celebrity's shoulder and nearly shed a tear. "I think Grand Camorra and I can work. Know what I'm saying? She's so fine and all; I'll treat this beauty like gold!"

Keyshawn was tickled.

"Why are you laughing?" Vern was confused. "Shouldn't you be pissed off at me? What gives, Keyshawn? I'm a backstabber."

"I think this may work out," said the television and movie star. "Vern, you rocked my boat that night, now realizing it was you and not Keyshawn. No man had ever given it to me like that. If that's how it is night in and night out, I have no other purpose in life than to be with you, Vern!"

"I need to record this declaration shit," said Vern. "Record us, Keyshawn. Wait! Don't close the bathroom door during my glory!"

Slam!

Grand Camorra added, "You seem like a nice guy, somebody who could protect me. I miss the thug in a man."

"It's all because I did it right!" Vern didn't mean to rub it in his friend's face, but he sure tried hard! He figured that if it costed his friend, it had to be. He had his dream lover! "This relationship opens up a ton of opportunities! Know what I'm saying? I don't have to live here and be working at some common man's workplace. Nope! You can take over the lease, Keyshawn. I'm moving out!"

"So basically you're going to use me to become a star?" asked Grand Camorra. "And aren't you moving too fast?"

"No!" Vern grabbed Grand Camorra by the neck and drilled the star's throat with his tongue! After he scooped soggy remnants of communion bread from her gums, he swallowed and shouted, "I love you! I'm done with everybody else, Rochelle and La Donna! They can all kick rocks!"

Keyshawn opened the bathroom door. "Congratulations."

"I knew that you'd come around to understand," said Vern. He popped Grand Camorra's buttocks with his hand.

Pop!

"I'm... happy... for you," laughed Keyshawn.

"What is so funny?" asked Vern. "Look at all the booty you're giving away to the truest player! She's going to twerk all night long! Dude, what in the hell is so funny? Keyshawn?"

"Okay, I hope that you're ready." Keyshawn held his breath. "Last Friday night, Vern, you helped yourself to a dude! Do you *know what I'm saying*? Huh?"

"Hey! What the fuck are you talking about?"

"Grand Camorra is a dude."

"Grand Camorra is not a dude!" shouted Vern. "I know the difference between a girl and a boy! Don't play that shit with me!"

"You didn't check," said Grand Camorra. "You just got me in that room and drilled me without any foreplay to know. Okay, I have a ding-o-ling."

"You had sex with a dude," stated Keyshawn.

"Technically," added Grand Camorra. "And I'm usually not that easy to persuade into the act. I just liked how you handled me."

Vern stood there and stopped breathing.

"Vern, I know. It was a shocker for me to find out she is a dude." Keyshawn shook his roommate. "I had never slept with Grand Camorra to know. Earth to Vern, hello? Are you alright, Vern?"

Suddenly, a huge smile grew upon Vern's face! "Well, whatever! As long as it feels as good as it felt the other night, I'm good with it! Know what I'm saying?"

"Ain't that about a bitch?" Keyshawn was shocked.

"Aye," said Vern, "the sex felt better than using my hand, and in the end, I got Grand Camorra! It's a miracle!"

Keyshawn shook his head and admitted defeat.

"Wait, does that make me bisexual since I like men and women?" Vern asked. "Well, I guess that's what I am! Just look at my girlfriend... I mean, boyfriend! Grand Camorra is hot as hell!"

"Well, I cannot say that I expected this." Grand Camorra wiped her shortened tears away and dropped her shoulders. She expected that the truth would lead to violence. Instead, as the pastor preached, the fact set everybody free.

"Believe it!" Vern danced. "Accept me, as your dude?"

"Vern, I accept!" Grand Camorra hugged Vern. "I'd love to get to know you and be your lover, after what I felt the other night. I do want to let you know that I do have plans for a sex change operation this winter. In the meantime, I'm still your dream girlfriend. We're now a couple, yes?"

"Yes, you'd better believe it!" Vern chuckled. "And about the coochie operation, I guess that's a bonus! In the meantime, let's talk and get to know one another in Paris or Spain. Can we fly away tomorrow?"

"It's your world, playa!" Keyshawn gave his boy a high five. "I guess that I cannot hate the player, but I'll hate the game. You're still my best friend. We'll talk about that Friday night incident another time because it was wrong, but for now, I'm glad you two work. Two problems are solved with one stone. Besides, Vern, you knew I was going to dump her anyhow; I wasn't feeling it."

"You were?" Grand Camorra was surprised.

"It was my parents that suggested we go to church," Keyshawn said, "and for me to fight through my miserable attitude I have. Just like them, nobody understands the pain I feel."

"Why have you been so miserable, Keyshawn?" Grand Camorra knew something was wrong with him but hadn't a clue why. "What's up with you, man? Just spit that shit out!"

166

Vern stated, "Sometimes, love just won't let go. That's what's up. He still has a thing for Veronica Evans. You, me, his parents, his co-workers, the press, and definitely Carl Cleveland have been in the way from him making up with her."

"I'm good now, though. At least somebody is happy." Keyshawn played it cool.

"I have an idea." Vern was dead serious. He knew that his friend was lied. "Aye Keyshawn, you need to get Veronica back! Know what I'm saying? I know that you love her a lot. And we both know that Carl is too damn old for her and a sell-out! You need to save her from that old joke. At least give it one last shot. It was, after all, mainly my fault to begin with that, you two broke up."

"How are you at fault?"

"I got you to speed that night, which got us pulled over and jailed; that set it off for her to leave you," Vern explained. "I'm sorry for calling you a chicken back then; you're a pretty solid dude. So, let me try to help fix things."

"How are you going to do that? She's with Carl Cleveland, every woman's dream, a romance god! Plus, he's got big ass bodyguards around him all the time."

Vern smiled. "Yeah, I think I've got a plan, as long as we've got star power on our side now. We also have Grand Camorra's bodyguards, so we're no longer outmanned. Know what I'm saying?

And Carl Cleveland is far from home. Baby, can you help me with getting my friend Keyshawn's lady back?"

"I think Keyshawn deserves a second chance," said Grand Camorra. "I'm sorry for deceiving you. You are a pretty neat guy, and I owe you too. I could tell that you weren't that interested after the movie set I did. I'm sorry for that too."

"Did you do that guy under the sheets on the set?"

"Those things are not for the public to know," answered Grand Camorra. "I will tell you that you can count on me to make up for all this. Let's get Veronica Evans back to you."

Chapter 14

Sometimes, Love Just Won't Let Go!

"Look."

"No, you look!" Veronica interrupted Carl. "I need to know the truth. What I saw in the studio has been on my mind for a bit. Then my old boss, Ms. Cobblestone, told me that you did it to her! Now, you had better not be lying! I'm not anyone's fool. You can bring me all these roses and chocolate, all you want, but I've never been the one to be played! Now, I want the truth, man. Come clean!"

Carl Cleveland stood outside of his limousine, which was parked in front of Veronica's home. "My goodness, baby, all I want to do is take you to a yoga class this morning. You're stressed out this morning, and you need a good stretching. It's only Monday; you start work in a few hours, so grab your workout bag and let's go!"

"Did you have sex with that ninety-year-old actress on the set or not? I want a yes or no, man!"

"I'm an actor. I'm supposed to convince you that it was real. That's what makes my romance movies sell."

"Is that a yes or no?"

"I'm an actor. I act. What do you think, woman?"

Carl's bodyguards and driver chuckled from the limousine.

Veronica pointed to his car. "I want you to get in your car and get the hell away from me!"

"Veronica! You're talking crazy and causing a scene! Now get your workout bag and get your ass in the car, so we're not late!"

"Who do you think you're talking to?" Veronica stood to Carl's face. "You don't be coming around here talking down to me unless you're ready to scrap! Carl, I dare you to say another word in that tone and watch what the hell happens."

"Look, I'm sorry. Okay? I just want to get in the car and stay on my schedule. Can you please come along?"

"Since you can't answer my question, hell no, I ain't going!"

The driver in the limousine hollered, "You've been as nice as you could to her, boss! Just leave her sorry ass if all she wants to do is fight! She's just a-ho-in-a-million!"

"Oh?" That angered Veronica. "So now I'm just-a-*ho*? As far as I know, Carl, you and I haven't done a damn thing. We haven't had sex, player? So, why do I have to be a *ho*? You're the one that broke muscles in your ass from all that sex you've done in your acting career. You're the *ho*! You're the one walking around dripping shit all over people's couches, and staining draws!"

"Aye, you need to keep my private business on the down-low! Okay? I don't want people out here hearing that, especially not the paparazzi. Calm the hell down, Veronica!"

"When was the last time you went to the doctors to get yourself checked out anyway? I have never heard of a man doing it so much that they broke muscles in their ass! Are you scared of something if you go? Maybe you've caught something like a disease."

"You don't have to do this," said Carl. "I want to be with you. I'm as nice as I can be to you. Now, you're starting to try my patience!"

"Is that all I'm doing? At least I'm not trying Ms. Cobblestone, my old boss! Carl, that's just nasty. She's got warts and all kinds of disgusting scents coming off her. Yeah, she told me all about your episode in the shower minutes before our last date. You and your bodyguards are quite a bunch of nasty whores. Uh-huh, you're busted, Carl! You're a low life piece of shit!"

"Shut up!" Carl suddenly grabbed Veronica by her wrist, while his bodyguards and his driver accompanied him in grappling her on the sidewalk. "Guys, throw her dumb ass in the car! I'm tired of being mister nice guy. No woman talks to me like this! It's time to set a bitch straight."

"Wait!" Veronica was in trouble. There were suddenly no witnesses that she saw, and a bodyguard placed his large palm over her mouth.

"Get your dumb ass in the car," said a bodyguard. He bowled her into the back seat like a piece of trash.

"Wait for nothing," said Carl. "I was nice to you, Veronica! It is women like you that take *the man* out of a man. All you had to do is give in a little. Your celebrity fame has erased you knowing how to work with a man, certainly Keyshawn, beneath you in status, didn't stand a chance. But with me, I'm the shit. Women will bow when I walk through the door and do as I say without argument!"

"Women kiss the ground that Carl Cleveland walks on!" One of the bodyguards held her down in the car. "And if they don't, he turns old school and slaps a whore! You've got the old Carl, now!"

"Veronica, do you think you are all that because you're a reporter?" Carl laughed. "I have treated you no less than a queen. You just don't know how to surrender or submit to a man, even when he submits to you. I gave you everything you wanted. But then a man gives you a little back and women like you take it for granted and try to either take it all over."

Veronica kicked at Carl!

"Or, you turn it into a requirement that we have to give, give, and give until there's nothing left of us!" Carl continued, "I was honest with you, since I've been with you, most of the time, but I'll be damned if I need to give or tell you everything I do. Not everything is your business! I'm a businessman; I don't just spill things!"

Veronica shouted, "You sure spilled all over my couch, you sick jerk! You're not going to get away with this, Carl!"

"This is a man's world!" Carl declared. "More importantly, this is my world! See, I run an organization on the side. Unlike your ex and his thug friends, probably related to a small street gang, I am the ultimate gangster. I employ police, government people, and court officials. I do not lose."

Veronica was defeated. Keyshawn had not seemed so bad after all. She realized that she had listened to everybody else instead of her own heart. She allowed her job to live her life. She did not trust in God's direction since she left the conference. All she did was crush a good man in Keyshawn. How she wished he was there to confront Carl and his goons because sometimes, love just wouldn't let go.

Carl continued to disappoint. "I guess that you just attract thugs. As if you haven't learned, we all love a good booty. And you surely have a nice one. But what matters now is who is going to stop me? I'm going to take you somewhere and teach you how to listen to your man. Now, put some tape over her mouth. She talks too much!"

Skurr! Vroom! A car roared from around the corner and headed straight towards Carl Cleveland's limousine! It had to been going over 45 miles per hour and nobody was in the driver's seat!

Carl thought the car looked familiar and shouted, "Everybody, get out of the limousine! Jump for it!"

One of Carl's bodyguards grabbed Veronica and dove to the sidewalk, along with his constituents.

Bash!

"What in the hell just happened?" Carl stood up from the sidewalk and saw that the 1978 Cutlass Supreme, which sat across half of his dashboard, totaled his limousine! A plastic rim rolled past him. "Who crashed that piece of garbage into my limousine?"

Another car suddenly sped up to the toasty scene in front of Veronica's luxurious home. It was another limousine!

Carl waved down that limousine, as he saw a dazed Veronica and his dizzy bodyguards on the ground. "Hey! Can we get some help over here? Hey! Thank you. Thank you for stopping."

The passenger window of the limousine slowly rolled down. Vern sat in the passenger seat and calmly asked, "Surely, you don't want *my* help. Know what I'm saying? Pull the car over for me, Frank."

"Wait a second. What in the world is going on here?" Carl watched that limousine park across the street. He graced his hands through his hair. "That's that little thug friend of Keyshawn!"

Vern got out of the limousine and stood to Carl's face. "Yeah, what's up now, dude? We got some talking to do about Veronica. Wait, why does she have tape over her mouth? You're trying to kidnap my homeboy's woman now?"

"You'd better get out of my face, you little punk!" shouted Carl. "All I have to do is yell that I'm being attacked, and nobody is going to help a thug beat me in any court. How about if I shoot you in self-defense? I'm sure that I would win that in court too."

Vern reluctantly backed up, as he felt the end of Carl's millimeter on his abdominal. "It's cool. Don't shoot me."

173

Veronica sat up and managed to spit the tape off of her mouth. "Don't shoot him, Carl!"

"No, it isn't cool!" shouted Carl. He cocked the gun. "I am the top black actor in film, and I have never come across this kind of disrespect in all of my years! I'm Carl Cleveland! Do you understand that player? You trashed my car and nearly killed us all!"

Veronica shouted, "Carl, I'll go with you! I'll do whatever you want! Please, don't shoot him!"

Carl was confused. "Which one of the thugs are you dating? You confuse me. Is it Keyshawn or his friend here? He seems to be the one that stands up like a man for your honor."

"Put the gun down!" Grand Camorra stepped out the back door of her limousine. She pointed her gun towards Carl's head.

"Are you kidding me?" Carl didn't move his gun away from Vern. "You're a woman! You don't have *the balls* to shoot me!"

Vern muttered, "Trust me, my woman *has* balls."

"Grand Camorra, bitch, you should be ashamed of yourself to be hanging around this narrow-minded thug," said Carl. "You get that gun out of my face! No? Wait a second. You're really into this thug. Wow! Listen, I didn't mean what I said the last time you attended the casting call. It probably could've been a great steamy scene if you had let me caress you at that time. Why won't you let a man get in that? I should! You're too hot to be into that imbecile!"

Vern was confused. "What's Carl talking about, baby?"

"I was cast as a double for a love scene with Carl," answered Grand Camorra, "but I refused to let him touch me inappropriately. So, I walked off the set."

Carl tried to pimp her. "You've got quite the body, Grand Camorra. Why don't you put down the gun? We can try again by you setting up an appointment for a private audition at my mansion next week in New York? I'm sure that we can start over and get you a leading role in my next movie. I'd like to test drive you!"

"That ain't happening!" Vern quickly kicked Carl's hand, but his foot caught the one without the gun!

Pop!

"No!" Keyshawn ran from around the corner of Veronica's home and jumped on Carl's back! He'd already let go of the love he had for his car; he was damned not to avenge his best friend! As Carl dropped his gun on the gutter, Keyshawn kneed and punched at Carl like there was no tomorrow. His knuckles instantly swelled up! Never in his life had he imagined to whoop on his teenage, action star icon.

Carl's bodyguards ran to assist him in removing Keyshawn, but Grand Camorra's bodyguards hopped out of her car to meet them in a clash of behemoths! Whoever spent more time in the weight room did most of the damage. They spotted the sidewalk with blood and teeth.

Police and ambulance sirens were heard not too far away.

Grand Camorra attended to Vern's bullet wound, which missed anything vital. He was okay but needed to stay still.

Veronica held onto Carl's leg, as Keyshawn dropped a few elbows on it. Carl screamed in agony as he lost control of his stool, and it sprinkled all over the lawn!

"You're going to respect women from now on!" screamed Veronica as she moved up from his dampened pants legs. She arrived at Carl's face, and power slapped him, nails and all, upside his head!

Whack!

Keyshawn pushed Carl down further into the lawn. "Hit him again, baby! Beat the shit out of this fool!"

Veronica shouted at Carl, "We're not just sperm banks, you sick bastard! We're human beings! How dare you mistreat women? But you were right about listening to my man. Keyshawn said to beat the shit out of you. So, guess what! I'm going to do that!"

"I love you, Veronica!" Keyshawn declared.

"Ah!" cried Carl. He was hopeless, as Veronica nearly choked his Adam's apple out and viciously slapped him more! "I'm sorry, Veronica! I got carried away! I'm so sorry! I can't breathe! Please stop it, Veronica! Please, don't kill me! I'm sorry!"

Pop! Pop!

Grand Camorra suddenly looked up. Carl Cleveland stopped

crying and looked up. The bodyguards all looked up. Vern looked around. Where did those gunshots come from?

Veronica and Keyshawn were sprawled over the sidewalk, motionless. Across the street in a parked car was Ms. Cobblestone with a smoking pistol.

"The end," she whispered and blew the gun smoke from the tip of her pistol. Revenge against Veronica was hers.

"Oh my goodness!" cried Grand Camorra. "She killed them!"

Ms. Cobblestone called out, "Carl Cleveland, let's go! Boys, help your movie star to the car and get in. Hurry up before the cops show up! Let's go!"

Ducking several rounds of bullets between Grand Camorra and Ms. Cobblestone, Carl hopped on one leg, assisted by his bodyguards, towards his ho's car. They all thankfully dove into the back seat.

"Roll the windows down back there!" Ms. Cobblestone shouted as she ducked Grand Camorra's bullets. "For the love of… Do you know that you smell like shit back there? Damn! Did you wipe your ass today, Carl?"

"I don't smell anything! Just drive the car!"

Skurr!

Ms. Cobblestone aggressively drove over corners, mowed

through mailboxes, and dodged magazine stands, as the emergency vehicles neared the area! She drove a couple more blocks when suddenly the manure odor tainted her sight like an onion! Carl's dirty ass odor ate up all the oxygen in the car! Ms. Cobblestone hyperventilated and fainted on the steering column!

Carl jumped out of that car the moment he noticed Ms. Cobblestone's brunette and gray hair draped over the dashboard! The horn blared when her head slammed into it.

Carl's bodyguards jumped out of the car and ran for it.

"Wake up!" screamed Carl. He could not help Ms. Cobblestone or steer the vehicle. He, too, jumped out the car and watched it drive right off a cliff!

The car went up in a mushroom cloud and fire, as Ms. Cobblestone sat up in flames like a prop and burned up. Her caked-on, oil-based make-up infuriated the fiery flames into a catastrophic explosion that was seen for miles.

Carl fled on foot in the direction, away from the cops. Flies and mosquitos chased after him and pecked at his dirty booty bite. He'd live to film again.

Meanwhile, back in front of Veronica's home, Grand Camorra continued to aid Vern. "The cops and ambulance are just about here! We've got to jet. Come on, baby."

Grand Camorra's bodyguards pulled her limousine up to her and Vern. Frank said, "Come on. We need to get out of here."

"This is my best friend," replied Vern. "I can't just leave them here. If I go down for this, which I shouldn't because I don't have a gun, just bail me out of jail later! Okay? Know what I'm saying? Now get out of here, so you don't get caught up in this mess! Go on!"

"You're a good dude," replied Grand Camorra. "I'm sorry about your friends. I'll come back for you when all of this crazy mess is over! Okay? I'll come back!"

Skurr! Grand Camorra's limousine roasted it out of that neighborhood. The scene was so jacked up that she wasn't sure if she'd ever return.

Vern sat there in front of his motionless friends. He called out,

"Keyshawn? Aye man, we done did it this time. Got' shot up by them jump out boys and stuff… Know what I'm saying?"

Suddenly, there was a movement from Keyshawn! Vern watched him struggle to his hands and knees.

"Aye Keyshawn, dude, I'm glad you're still with me!" Vern was happy to see his friend moving after being shot in his head. "I thought you ate it! Know what I'm saying? I don't know if Veronica made it. She hasn't moved at all; I couldn't feel a pulse. I think she's gone. I'm sorry, Key."

Keyshawn did not respond to Vern.

"Aye, are you okay?" Vern asked. "Keyshawn, come on, man. Damn! Man, I love you! Dude, it's time for you to go on home now. Know what I'm saying? It's time to let go."

Vern hovered, as he watched his friend crawl towards Veronica. Keyshawn moaned as if he had things left to say. He could not articulate any words. His heart was near death, as his brain spoke from his soul and willed his body over the lawn.

Vern cried out as he watched his best friend crawl to his true love, Veronica Evans. The only thing left in Keyshawn's dying body was a few beats in his heart, which were reserved *only* for Veronica.

She was the spark in his life, no matter what her family, co-workers, friends, church gossipers, and counselors thought or saw otherwise. Keyshawn knew his woman behind closed doors and vice-versa; that was where the real relationship took place. Everybody else in Keyshawn and Veronica's business had it all wrong.

Five police cars rolled up to the scene, nothing but commotion and sirens blaring. A lot of police stepped from their vehicles and pointed their pistols towards Vern, Keyshawn, and Veronica.

"Everyone, freeze, in the name of the law!" shouted the police.

"We surrender!" shouted Vern. He painfully raised his arms high and then recognized that some police were the very same officers that pulled Keyshawn and himself over the night they ran over that pig. "You guys need to put the guns away! We need medical attention! They are dying over there! Help them, please!"

"The ambulance is on its way," replied the sadistic cop.

"Hey! I don't hear any ambulance sirens anymore! What happened to the ambulance?"

"Isn't that something?" asked the police officer. "If it isn't Richard Whiteman... That is your name, isn't it, boy?"

Vern recognized that bastard and disappointedly shook his head. "Come on, man. You've got all these police and guns! Know what I'm saying? And I know that you've gotten over a fucking joke! Know what I'm saying? It was a joke, man! Help my friends!"

"I am not a pig!" shouted the cop, who stroked his chin stubble. "It appears that you're on my side of town now, boy. Your kind has never been welcomed out here. Veronica was our token. Well, it appears to me that you and your gangster friend came over to this side of town to start problems. We've got that piece of trash of a car crashed into a very nice limousine there and bullet shells over here."

"Man... we are shot! Know what I'm saying? We're dying and shit!" Vern cried. "Call for some medical help or something! Know what I'm saying, you bitch-made mother fucker!"

"Hey, you over there!" shouted the vengeful cop, who pointed his gun at Keyshawn. "You stop crawling to that girl! I thought that I told you to freeze! I said freeze!"

Vern quickly dropped his arms, picked up Carl Cleveland's gun from the gutter, and ran in Keyshawn's direction! "No, don't shoot! Don't shoot!"

Pop! Pop! Pop! Pop! Pop! The cops opened fire at Keyshawn, but Vern took all the slugs when he dove in the way! Vern wasn't going out like a punk and fired off his gun at the cops while he ascended to the concrete! *Pop! Pop! Pop! Pop! Pop!*

Cop cars blew up in fiery explosions and a wall of murderous flames, as Vern slid headfirst through the lawn!

Amidst the surrounding fire, Keyshawn continued to crawl towards his lover slowly. Not even *hell on earth* could stop him from reaching his love. Blood fell from his mouth, and his dimming gray pupils set upon Veronica. When he finally made it, he exhaustively fell upon her. What a taxing ride, an unnecessary adventure he had with his woman that ended early because of jealous or uninformed opinions on every side. Keyshawn's tired and bloody tongue hung from his opened mouth; he sailed on.

Shaking with inevitableness, Veronica tightly wrapped her arms around Keyshawn and took one last gasp of our nasty, filthy, jealous, racist, cruel, pro-divorce, confused, and sinful world. She entirely and finally understood the genuine love he had for her. Then she found herself reaching for his outstretched hand within the majestic abundance of eternity because their love just wouldn't let go.

However, she could only salvage a little hope to sail on with Keyshawn because, like her, our world subscribed to such atrocities: *Nothing lasts forever,* and the 1662 Book of Prayers bull jive out of England that reads '*Til death do you part.*'

The truth of the matter was that Veronica and Keyshawn weren't married, so there was a chance that she'd never see Keyshawn ever again, even in eternity. Yet, she tightly held onto him, hoping in love, to sail alongside him on his heavenly voyage.

Apologetic and sorrowful with her final thoughts, she finally realized that she had a good thing from the start with Keyshawn. There she laid, shot dead on the open lawn, as her foot caught on fire. Together, Veronica, Keyshawn, and Vern lit up in large flames that soared to the heavens.

If only Veronica had listened to her man and nobody else: Those jealous-ass friends, the co-workers, and over-protective parents that continued to say that she could do better. They honestly never knew Keyshawn before they judged him!

After a flash of her entire life, she recognized his genuine love for her in death. Veronica tried to chase Keyshawn in eternity, but he sailed away with his thug homeboy, Vern.

Time was not present in death, so wounds never healed. Veronica eventually drowned with the rest of the misdirected women on earth that never saw the good in their men. There, they all mildewed and rusted, in a miserably dark, empty, and the blackest sea of wasted souls that forever cried over and over that sometimes, love just won't let go.

By Ashaki Boelter

Sometimes, Love Just Won't Let Go

978-0-9796219-9-4